EXHIBITIONS

EXHIBITIONS

Tales of Sex
in the City

edited by Michele Davidson

ARSENAL PULP PRESS
Vancouver

ARSENAL PULP PRESS
103 - 1014 Homer Street
Vancouver, B.C.
Canada V6B 2W9
www.arsenalpulp.com

The publisher gratefully acknowledges the support of the
Canada Council for the Arts and the B.C. Arts Council for its
publishing program, and the Department of Canadian
Heritage through the Book Publishing Industry Development
Program for its publishing activities.

The Canada Council | Le Conseil des Arts
for the Arts | du Canada

Canadä

Typeset by Solo
Printed and bound in Canada

CANADIAN CATALOGUING IN PUBLICATION DATA:
Main entry under title:
  Exhibitions

  ISBN 1-55152-078-8

1. Erotic stories. I. Davidson, Michele.
PN6120.95.E7E94 2000   808.83'93538   C00-910250-7

Contents

Acknowledgements

This anthology was truly a labour of love. Unless thousands upon thousands of you purchase a copy, I'll never retire on its royalties. That's fine by me. The editing experience was more meaningful to me than any cheque.

There are a number of people who deserve acknowledgement. Brian Lam and Blaine Kyllo at Arsenal for their faith, and for showing me the ropes; Katja Pantzar for opening Arsenal's door by introducing me to Blaine; and my hiking buddy Bob Sabiston for helping to keep me sane.

Most significantly, I thank my remarkable parents, Ron and Gail Davidson. It really is impossible to express how grateful I am to you both for nurturing my independent spirit, and for encouraging me to do more than just dream. All children should be so blessed.

Foreword

DEBBIE STOLLER

READING EROTICA IS A LOT LIKE READING A TRAVELOGUE: it allows you to imagine a place, or a person, that you might never experience first hand. So when Michele Davidson invited me to write the foreword for a compilation of erotic stories she was working on, I was ready to go along for the ride. And go for a ride, I did. It took me a long time to read through all the stories that Michele sent me. Not because there were so many of them, or because they were so long, but, well, let's just say I couldn't get through them all at once. I would read, get turned on, jerk off, take a nap. Then I'd get started reading again. There were, to be sure, a lot of really hot stories in the mix.

But I went for a ride in another way, too, because in each of the tales in this collection, place plays as important a role as person. Even more interestingly, the stories cross geographical terrain as easily as they traverse the landscape of sexual preferences. And, as with a travelogue, you don't find yourself looking for stories written from your same sexual perspective any more than you look for stories that take place in your home town. It's the voyage to other places, other sexual preferences, that excites.

The stories took me everywhere. While reading one, I could suddenly visualize sex through the eyes of a heterosexual man as he slipped his fingers beneath a woman's skirt on a crowded Tokyo train. Reading another, I could take on the role of a gay man, and travel to Venice, where a young man glances at me in a way that makes my dick hard. I could also transform myself into a man giving head to his boyfriend in a garden behind the cool stone walls of the Cloisters, or a gay woman who gets wet as she watches an ex-girlfriend finger-fuck a new lover via surveillance cameras at a U.S.

mint. Via the nimble pen and vivid imaginations of the writers selected for this compilation, I can picture each of these experiences almost as readily as I can fantasize about my own sexual preferences, that of your everyday, dime-a-dozen straight girl.

I was already familiar with one of the stories in the collection. Nell Carberry's "Night Train" was the first in a series of stories we began publishing in *BUST* a few years ago. To make it clear what the purpose of the stories were, we gave them an obvious title: One-Handed Read. These were not stories to be read on the subway on the way to work. These were stories you were meant to read in the bathtub, in your bed, or over the phone to a special someone. As the title suggested, the idea was that you could hold the magazine open with one hand, and leave your other hand free for … other pursuits.

I suppose that publishing an erotic story in a feminist magazine wouldn't be an obvious choice for most editors. But at *BUST*, which is intended to be a fierce and funny alternative to mainstream women's magazines, it was a necessity. We figured that, since men's magazines were always full of wall-to-wall women, we owed it to our female readers to deliver them some eye candy, too. But rather than stick to pull-out spreads of a naked Burt Reynolds or other hairy-chested manly men, as *Cosmopolitan* had chosen to do a few decades back, we'd give the girls something they could actually get turned on by: a sexy story.

In choosing the stories for our One-Handed Read, I have always been very careful to select from a variety of perspectives. I did not want to be limited to printing endless, stereotypical female fantasies, laden with bodice ripping and plenty of cuddling. After all, one of the most interesting things about erotica is its ability to take you outside of the boundaries of everyday experience. "Night Train," with its story of a woman who gets bound up and fucked by a practical stranger on a New York City subway train, was the perfect place for us to start: it was hot, unexpected, and anything but politically correct.

Since then, we've printed stories about a woman whose boyfriend wants her to do him with a dildo, and another that presents an erotic encounter between two surfer boys, in which the only female present is the author of the story. Not surprisingly, the One-Handed Read has been an unbridled success and is one of the most-read features of the magazine. Not every reader gets turned on by every story we print, but that's exactly the point. There is no single type of sexy story that all women, all men, all straights, all gays, or all bisexuals will respond to. The dominatrix by day may find herself at nightfall most turned on by the innocent tale of a man who misses his wife; the straight-as-an-arrow man might get a rise from the story of a somewhat violent encounter between an old Italian queen and a young male tourist. After all, reading erotica is about exploring and discovering the contours of your unique, sexual self.

Like the stories we publish in *BUST*, the tales in *Exhibitions* are proof that pleasure knows no politics, and that the sexual imagination knows no bounds. And, like any good travel story, they can take you places you may never have been, all from the comfort of your own home. And the stories are better than mere travelogues, because even though you may never get to go to any of these places in real life, at least you'll get to come.

Introduction

MICHELE DAVIDSON

I WAS TWENTY-FIVE WHEN I READ Anaïs Nin's *The Delta of Venus*. It changed the way I looked at my body and my sexuality. Nin's writing awakened in me the realization that sex is as natural and necessary a part of life as eating and breathing. I was inspired to explore, question, and experiment. Erotica became part of that adventure.

Reading erotic literature opened my eyes to the wonderful and varied forms of sexual expression. Sex between women. Sex between men. Heterosexual sex. Multi-partner. Solo. BDSM. Fetish practices. And yes, exhibitionism. Writers who can evoke experiences provide an endless supply of details for the imagination, and I discovered that the experience, regardless of gender or activity, is what arouses.

Erotica blurs the boundaries of sexual expression. A good writer can, through their use of language, allow the reader to step into the skin of another and experience something new. When I first read a story about a homosexual experience written from the male perspective, I was astonished by my body's arousal response. I already knew that literature could take me down roads I'd never travelled, and to visit cultures about which I knew little, but the realization that it could be a vehicle to my own sexual liberation took me by surprise.

What Nin awakened, further readings of erotic literature ripened. I happily discovered that I needn't be ashamed of my vivid and experimentally rich sexual fantasies. Other women and men had these fantasies, too. So when sexually naïve girlfriends talked about being stranded on a desert island with a dark, handsome hunk, I no longer cringed in embarrassment to reflect on my comparatively twisted ideas.

Thus I began one of my life's greatest journeys – an expedition of sexual discovery that eventually led me towards a deeper understanding of my self. Not only as a sexual creature, but as a mindful, empowered, and fulfilled woman. I realize now that unflinching sexual honesty and examination are part of something much bigger. Our entire being benefits from reflection and effort. In this, sexual growth is no different from other forms of personal growth.

Today, those who know me best know of the joy I take in exploration. Of my reverence for the beauty, the passion, and the poetry of life. I see my sexuality as existing interdependently with the other aspects of my self. Together these bring me to an appreciation of my existence. Making it meaningful includes embracing varied sexual experiences.

My sexual empowerment really began with Nin's example of the intelligent expressive woman, and erotica's implicit permission to give myself the gift of sexual experimentation. Without these, much of my sexual nature would remain under lock and key today, alive only in my imagination.

Thankfully, my journey of sexual discovery was well under way when a couple of particularly sexy stories stimulated my curiosity about exhibitionism. Through good luck, or good karma, I was fortunate at this time to have a partner who also sought to examine and understand our sexuality.

This wonderfully open lover and I used erotica as a stepping stone to develop our interest in exhibitionism. Churches, airports, apartment hallways, balconies. We read about them. We did them. I will always cherish the thrilling memories of our shared sexual escapades. I've continued what he and I began by having erotic experiences in many of the countries I've travelled to since. Even in my hometown of Vancouver.

So it was that after years of reading erotic stories, I decided to write my own. Writing about my fantasies was – and is – an exhilarating side trip in my ongoing sexual explorations.

It was while writing a piece about sex in Indonesia that I realized many of my pieces share a common theme: exhibitionism. I thought back to those sexy stories that so turned my lover and I on. I remembered how much fun we had re-enacting scenes from the stories and playing out some of our own. And how we both felt a sense of freedom through taking these risks. It was then I first thought that compiling a collection of erotic tales, set in places readers could easily imagine or even visit for themselves, would be an interesting project. An erotic tour guide of sorts.

Religious followers retrace the steps of martyrs. History buffs recreate famous battles. I like to think of *Exhibitions* as a tool for sexual pilgrims who seek to discover and invent, with a little titillation along the way.

When enjoying sex in a public place, you never know if someone will come stumbling around a corner, interrupt your escapade, catch you in the act. The idea that, at any moment, you could be discovered, adds to the intensity of the experience. In the same way, reading erotic literature is exciting because a reader never knows whether the story actually happened, or is just a construct of a writer's aroused imagination. I leave it to you to wonder about the stories in *Exhibitions*.

Like Nin, I believe that curiosity plays a huge role in our passions. The more curious, the more willing we are to ask questions, explore, and experiment – the more fun we have. Travel excites our curiosity about place, and erotica stimulates our sexual curiosity. Erotic stories that evoke a sense of place really stir us up.

It's been a dozen years since I first read *The Delta of Venus*. Nin's pioneering spirit continues to inspire me to explore, fantasize, role-play, and take erotic risks. Sexuality is my magnetic north. With or without a partner, being in touch with my sexual nature keeps me on course. Good erotic literature helps me navigate.

The stories in *Exhibitions* are intended to feed your passionate nature – some by causing you to think deeply about your own sexuality, and about what constitutes a sexual experience; others by arousing you physically. They may also encourage you to visit Montparnasse Cemetery in Paris, ride a night train in New York, or tour the Opera House in Sydney. All, I hope, will *stimulate* your sense of adventure.

Four Views of Mount Fuji

From the apartment's little window

I LOVE JAPAN. No, not a total, complete, blind kind of love. I've got
a clear sight of her blemishes, her flaws. She is not the perfect mis-
tress, but, still, she does the job. Cool, tranquil, precise, elegant.
There is something there that touches me. I imagine walking down
quiet streets busy with smiling masks, chaotic with brilliant *kanji* –
feeling an affinity, an excitement.

I dream of Japan, but not too complete a fantasy. I know enough
to capture a half-truth, a partial idea of reality – the details that only
a blind lover might see. So, I get things wrong; I make mistakes in
my personal illusions. But fantasies aren't supposed to be too real. I
enjoy them just the way they are, with blemishes, flaws. Enough to
be hot, not enough to be blindly, neurotically perfect.

On a futon, in a tiny apartment. Highway out the small window,
low hill, distant clouds, and the slopes of the great mountain.
Hokusai comes to mind, my own view of Mount Fuji. Murakowa is
her name, and for someone from a doll land she is not ubiquitous,
which is why she is daring when she's alone with me, the bearded
gajin, the foreign devil in her precise country. You wouldn't see it,
but she does, they do, and I do – a few extra pounds, breasts too
large, too plump. Too short in a land of bonsai and perfect minia-
tures. Small, heavy, she is not the elevator-girl, the cookie-cutter
view of marriageable perfection. In my fantasy, she has a giggling
fever about her, a genie released from too tight confinement. Too
many years being an ugly duckling, but in this place, this strange
gajin's apartment, she can be a swan.

On the streets, eyes downward, small steps. Here, in this very
expensive, very small apartment, she explodes. We kiss, mixing

breaths. My hands on her body, the body that she's been told to hate, but that to me is precious and exciting. I'm not a saviour, but giving in to lust feels good. My cock is hard, pressing through the thin cotton of my pants. Her breasts, her shame, are heavy, hanging, tipped by large nipples. I bend to taste, to sample, and find them salty – filling my mouth with a plump, firm knot. First the right, then the left, each kiss, each suck making her high, musical voice reach new octaves, new melodies.

With her facing the window, big breasts resting on the sill, staring out at the distant haze, the very distant mountain, I stroke her back and cup the twin mounds of her ass. Tight and firm, tensed from shivers of sensation and anticipation. I gently part them, surprised at her willingness, and run a single finger front (downy hair) to back (puckered asshole), fondling with my solitary stroke the fat lips of her cunt. Again, a little firmer touch, more insistent, and I feel those lips part, ever so slightly. Again, and my pass is faster, lubricated by juices that I can't quite feel. Again, and a small hand reaches down to take mine, to push me up, inside. Heat, like a small kettle on a long fire. Wet, like warm soapy water. Satin, like folds of a fine dress. Deep within, and – above me, looking out at her own view of Mount Fuji – she moans and almost cries.

I bow down to her neglected shrine and taste sweet. I taste the dark earthiness of her asshole next, the base with the celestial. But I know what she wants, what I want. In fantasies, any position is easy, never causes cramps, never makes the back of my neck ache. So this is not a concern as I bend under her and take her sweet clit between my soft lips. There, that magic spot for her and for me – the bead of her ecstasy in my mouth.

She screams her delight, and then her release, to the distant slopes of Mount Fuji.

On the stage, in the club
I had some friends who lived this way and it has always fascinated me. The foreigners in their land, paid to perform on stage. I have this lady friend, an occasional lover. Wouldn't, the fantasy goes, that be exotic enough – lanky me, with skin the colour of old cream; and her with polished black skin, large breasts, and lumpy ass? Wouldn't that attract the attention of some cabaret owner, entice him enough to give us enough to live in that other world?

The stage – more of a runway. A narrow strip of firmly anchored plywood painted with thick coats of vinyl paint. The walls are mirrored, shot with gold veins. In the ceiling, a clotted constellation of pinspots. The place is cool, but not cold. Sometimes I imagine snow outside, a static of softly falling flakes. Sometimes it's just bitterly cold, a chilly slap that rolls into the club every time a patron enters or exits.

The announcer is short and stocky, eyes hidden behind *yakuza* shades. I don't speak the language, but always feel a slight bite of anger at his mocking tones, his giggling introduction. Still, I remind myself, running a hand down my lover's back as we wait in the narrow wings, the audience hasn't come, hasn't paid, to laugh at his bad jokes.

To some old tune, some forgotten top ten, we walk onto the stage. Me, knowing a few words, parrot a joke at my own expense. Still, I am the star, and the charge is obvious. There might be shame, as I drop my kimono, revealing my hard, naked self, but it is also a kind of accolade. We are the stars here, and they wouldn't be there, sitting in silence, if they didn't want in some way what we do every night.

As my lover takes my cock in her mouth, kneeling down on a convenient piece of foam padding, I groove on their power, the silent salarymen. The businessmen concluding a deal, the few pervs – their hunger coming over me in waves of lust.

She sucks me, feeling their eyes on her. Such a perv herself, rolling in their disgust and envy. She is so alien to them, so different. Fat, in a land where size and health are always related to behaviour. Fat means you are bad. Handicaps are evidence of some wrong-doing. Black, where you are nothing if you are not Japanese. Sexual, where the mask preserves and protects everyone.

So, the fantasy goes, she sucks me on stage. She has a strong scent, and after a point it tickles my nose, a silent signal honed from many nights, much practice. I turn and make another joke, again in a language I do not speak, and she turns away, still stroking my cock, to feign a blush.

Then she turns and shows herself off to them, as the bad comedian makes jokes from the darkness. Holding her great breasts before them, like the fonts of all life. She pulls on her dark nipples, pinching them as she pushes her great hips forward – a pelvic scoop towards their straining cocks. They are rapt, staring at the tangle of her bush as it pushes out towards them.

On cue, she kneels down, bends at her soft belly till she is on all fours – brown eyes looking out at their calm masks. We change every so often, to keep the regulars just that. But this one is easiest. Some of the more acrobatic positions are wonderful for casual fucking, but for stage exhibitionism they can tear up the back, the knees.

And so, in the club, before their rapt eyes, I fuck her. Slide my cock into her hot, wet cunt. It embraces me, and for another night I know that this is a show as much for her and for me. We fuck, her groans half real and half acting, but I know that even she doesn't know where performance and reality separate. Sometimes she comes, a rarity, but it's a treat for us and another verification for me.

As the male star of this exotic zoo show, I try to come most nights – pulling my hard cock out of her hot wetness to shoot very Japanese-looking come onto her so-dark ass. Sometimes, though, I fake it, too – a bull-roaring orgasm owing more to Kirk Douglas overacting than to my real climax.

To their constant and tempered applause we bow, celebrities on stage for just the moment – but more than likely the stars of their fantasies for many days to come.

————

In a car, looking out over the city
Sometimes they're places of satisfaction, a kind of erotic home you can come back to time and again. But sometimes fantasies are places to think about what you wouldn't ever do.

For someone who likes Japan, I have very un-Japanese desires. I like dark … no, black skin. I like big women, broads who act their mind and let their desires take control once in a while. Not very Nippon.

Still … I think about this sometimes, trying on new shoes to see if they fit: a new dream to possibly add to my catalogue of fantasies.

She's young, but old enough. A schoolgirl icon. Unlike many of my fantasies, she doesn't have much of a background, not much realism to additionally flesh her out. She exists like a totem dropped from the Japanese collective consciousness into the passenger seat of my car. The Schoolgirl. Doe eyes and plaid skirt. Tiny white shoes, tiny white socks. A simple white blouse and a tie marking her educational institution.

She hides her porcelain face behind delicate hands as I pass my fingers across her tight thighs. "You're beautiful," I tell her in my suddenly good Japanese.

She giggles, a cotton-candy sound, a Hello Kitty melody of shyness. But she doesn't scream, doesn't pull away.

Out the front windshield are the lit windows of Tokyo – the myriad little glowing squares revealing people's lives. It's like a great monster's attention, a Godzilla with a million eyes, watching our every movement.

Never one to disappoint, I reach over and knead her small breasts, feeling her hard nipples through the simple bra. I am shocked, pleased, that they are so large, easily coins, though I don't know the denomination yet. She moans, pulling slightly away, but not enough to completely break contact with my hand.

With my other I return to her thigh, kneading the tight muscles, enjoying the silk of her skin. I try and part them, pulling gently but persistently on her leg, but she gives a chirp of disapproval, so I stop – changing my focus to her breast, to the nipple that I can now see as a shadow rise on her blouse, even in the dim light cast by those distant windows.

I know she can see it too, know that her cunt is growing hot, wet from my hand as well as the city's distant eyes. The stage might be small for this girl, but she's on it nonetheless: standing proud, eager to be seen and to show more.

The blouse parts, buttons slipping free under my feverish, yet skilled fingers. So young, so cherry, for a beat of my throbbing heart I can't tell skin from silk, the two luxuriously similar. Quickly, I rub a finger across the roughness of her bra, feeling the tight knot of that nipple. Entranced by those staring windows, she does not giggle, does not pull away. Instead, she grips the side of the seat, as if expecting to be lifted up, flown through the windshield and out into the hungry city.

She doesn't resist this time. No, she is fluid, melting under my hands, fingers, their eyes. Her thighs part, swinging wide, and in the dim light cast by those windows, her panties shine pure white. Brusquely, feeling her excitement, I dip a finger down. Smooth skin, with only a hint of hair, fuzz. Smooth and – pushing down farther, back – wet. So wet. Not just slick, not just damp. A wetness.

She was moaning before, soft, almost quiet. But now she cries, the sweet little sobs not of sadness but of screaming desire. Her hips start to buck, start to eagerly fuck my finger, rubbing her clit on my knuckle.

Feeling her start, feeling her cunt grip, grip, and grip again around my finger, I reach with my other, free, hand and grip that small breast, cup it, then squeeze hard – clutching the tenderness in my strength, pushing her up and over.

Her tears and screams echo around the confines of the car, bouncing around like a rubber ball thrown hard. I don't stop, and instead knead and fuck her even harder, pushing her over and over and over again. Finally, when the tears start to sound like those of discomfort, I stop.

She sleeps like an angel, curling in the smooth embrace of the seat, pale legs glowing in the distant lights. I pat her head, feeling a soft tickle of hair. She coos like a contented cat as I start the engine, pull out into the cool light. After a point, I have to watch the road and not her, but I know in this dream that they, from those thousands of windows, are still looking, appreciating.

On the train, during rush hour
To ride the legend. To be pressed into the bullet train, blasting through ancient countryside in state-of-the-art technology. I long to experience the sociological compression, the polite confinement of the salaryman's commute. The landscape a blur of green, brown, and shimmering steel. The floor of the train trembling with velocity. The sickly sweet tones of the automated destination announcer. I crave them all.

The air is light with perfume and sedate cologne. We, all of us, are part of some great collective organism, swaying, jostling with a single-minded biological urge . . . not to touch, much, and to get home as quickly as possible.

Or so I've heard. I've also heard rumours, stories of the train, of salarymen with their heads buried in bondage and rape comics as flesh-and-blood schoolgirls stand next to them, reading their textbooks.

Maybe it's this surface tension, stretched too tight between elaborate fantasy and too-firm reality. The id of media, the superego of work, responsibility, the face. The nail that stands up gets pounded down – so you don't stand up, you just bend, and keep on bending.

The word itself is lost to me, but the concept is there. Not really my cup of tea, but the concept is fascinating, enough for me to imagine it, and feel the tension in my cock rise.

Face. The mask is all. The role, appearance, is everything. It must be preserved against embarrassment, against standing out. It's a strong force, a cohesive, binding element of Japanese society.

But, still, this is me, and even in fantasy I must have an element of permission. So let's add some eye contact where it doesn't exist, a flirt with the eyes, a pursing of lips. She's an idol model, a hip bodi-con (body conscious) girl – one of the new Japanese girls with money, time, and a sexuality that is finally allowed release.

Coming back from a night wandering from one club to another, dancing under twirling lights. Tired, high, and excited. Maybe the train is having an effect. She, the flamboyant girl, the one burning with sexuality in a land where the mask keeps it firmly in place for everyone else. A latex dress that shows off her girlish, but still womanly figure, a pair of fancy black shoes. Hair flamboyant.

My hand on her thigh. We're shoved together, people next to people next to people. Crowded as only a society that employs professional "pushers" to cram just a few more passengers into each car can be.

And my hand is on her thigh. Oh, sure, she could pull away; she could certainly slap me away. Absolutely, she could spit something nasty in her high, fluty voice. But she doesn't. She doesn't move closer, and she doesn't pull away.

Bodi-con or no, the mask is there. The preservation of cool and dignity in the face of everything. It rolls through her mind, a choice of hells: a private, personal one where this *gajin* puts his huge hairy hand on her thigh, or the public one of showing a reaction, making a scene.

Besides . . . well, maybe the choice is not so absolute. Maybe there's another force at work in her elegantly narrow eyes. A firm, strange hand just inches from her cunt, dance-beat pulse still rocking through her body. The high of the clubs, the taste of the sexual undercurrent. The faceless bodies around her, trapped in their social insulation.

She doesn't pull away. My hand gets higher. Silken, firm thighs. Toned muscles. Hot. For a moment I relish that feeling, a special kind of heat: part inside of a latex dress, part crowded train, part . . . she moves a little closer.

Soft, smooth skin – then satin. I know, then, there, that I have reached the goal, the nirvana of every salaryman on that train. A hovering layer of fine material between by fingers and her wet cunt. Again, I hover, enjoying the summit, just within sight of the peak.

I am not eager to penetrate. That's not the point. It's not a goal-driven thing. Just to be there, amid all this normality, this average-ness, no matter now exotic, and have that connection, that permission. She and I: not really lovers, not really friends, but not strangers either. Standing there, my hand against the heat of her panty-covered cunt, we are different from those others around us. Our heat is because of them, though, because of the need to preserve face, to keep the mask intact.

Sometimes, when I think of this, I imagine slipping a finger between satin underwear and body and feel her heat, her wetness, maybe even the tight, hard bead of her clit. Other times, though, I just relish in that intimate connection and it's enough.

It's enough that we stand there, relishing in our heat, amid all those cold and reserved faces.

The Traveller is Lost

NATALEE CAPLE

MY DEAR JULIE,

This morning on my walk I watched a house catch fire. I was walking down the empty road, staring at my black shoes turning brown with dust, and something made me turn and stare through the shimmer of heat. I knew that I should be in the Gulf Hotel, working at my desk, constructing a virtual version of this day and of this place to wire around the world. I looked back at a house that I had just passed and I saw nothing, just a flat roof and some broken windows. Then it seemed as if the roof were rising. I thought I saw black birds escaping, but it was smoke and ash, and in the time that it took for the dark transformation of those birds the house suddenly caught – struck like a giant match, and it was blazing in the middle of the morning beside an empty street. Blazing away and all the air above it turned black and I thought of the bedsheets catching fire inside and writhing across the mattress, and the white pillows smoking, and the curtains evaporating. I thought of your necklace with the cherry wood beads. I thought of a song that I memorized in high school. I thought of the little plastic boat that used to float in the tub with you, holding your perfume and your scented oil. I thought of you sitting in the tub with your face flushed and your hair in a ponytail, and you covering your small teeth to laugh. I stood and I watched the house fall in upon itself the way that my thoughts were falling in upon themselves. I felt thirsty and my eyes stung.

Here, I should tell you, crows fly into ruined houses and spend the night. My easy rhetoric does not dispel the ashes. In the day there are loud noises that you would find unbearable, and I have become somewhat hopeless at my job. The waves break before the shore and I imagine what it must be like to live here always, drifting through the hot and noisy days and sleeping through the quiet dreadful nights and feeling no ambition, no ambivalence beyond the war. It seems as if people have ceased to be like living things, like animals, and now we only tread through time. We are detached from ourselves. Every action and reaction here has politics. And so you think, before you buy three bananas and a loaf of bread, whether it is right. Do I need three bananas today or should I buy just one and another tomorrow? Should I buy twenty? What will happen?

I've watched my neighbours burying their valuables in the gardens at night, all of them together, digging under the fragile illumination of their flashlights. Hiding necklaces, and wedding rings, dollar bills in paper bags. There is something hopeful in these burials. The families must be thinking that they will return. They must be thinking that the houses will burn but the gardens will be tilled again, and underneath the scrub, and earth, and broken stones, precious things will remain precious.

Far away from here you must be treading through your kitchen now, fixing yourself dinner. You must be drawing down the bowls and turning on the stove. You must be singing to yourself. What's that? A lullaby? You sing every song so slowly I can't tell. If you only knew how the tiny silent spotlight of my vision brightens around your wrist as you lift the strands of silk from the bared beads of corn. If you only knew how my fingers ache to touch your throat when you are singing. Far away from me you must be licking the salt from your upper lip and the melted butter from your thumb. Are you there? Where are you? When I finally called yesterday there was nothing, no you, with whom to speak. I so long to hear you breathe, to hear you shift and lean against the wall. To know that my voice is in your hair and that your mouth is nearby. I found myself thinking today that I wish you would write and say that you are pregnant. Not that I want a child, because I don't and never will, but because it would give me some reason, some absolute reason to come home. So write and tell me about this miracle and then meet me at the airport and shake your head and laugh because it is not true. There is only me and there is only you. I can see the look on your face as you read what I have just written. You smile and shrug your shoulders and your forehead bunches with sadness. It stings my heart to touch your nerves this way. But it is nice the way that a letter can collapse time and make it seem as if you are in front of me, reacting to my words even as I print them.

There is another journalist in the room connecting mine and twice now we have gotten drunk. He has crimson-tasselled curtains and we drink white rum from every teacup that remains unbroken. He pats his distended belly after every sip. Julie, how can I write to you about this place when all I can see are the white rafters over your head and the maple leaves scraping the window glass? Here, the smell of gunpowder reminds me of the smell of pencil shavings. It hangs everywhere and it clings to the bristles in my nose at every breath. I cannot sleep, for every rustle in the street wakes me and my heart batters my ribs like a bird in a box. I find all my bedsheets and my clothes stiff with the last night's sweat. The other journalist types constantly, a rat-tat-tat of trenchant thoughts tumbling down the hall. I hear him laugh and pull on his shoes to go out walking. I see in his eyes, the way that he captures and deconstructs whatever is before him. What I say is at once what I say, and also some great unfastening of me. His restless fingers flex and tap as he listens. He always hands me something, like rum or bread, when he asks me questions. I speak to him of the great gap that I feel between what people say they believe and what people actually think. I ask him: how can we report the dull horror of these days and the prickling nausea of these nights, as if they were important, when all we must do is report them? I confess my homesickness, and that I can no longer concentrate on the tedious unravelling of every struggle. I believe that human callousness is a crime. But I can think only of you, Julie.

When the tanks roll down the street I turn my head and watch the frames of my glasses shudder on the table by my bed. The universe quivers and all the sleepers wake. I count a thousand seconds of silence. I watch my glasses vibrate until they begin to turn. Last week I was buying fruit and bread at the edge of a road leading into the country. I was standing with a hand in my pocket, touching the leather of my wallet. A boy was looking at me, holding out his hand for me to place some money in it. That brown boy was looking at me. We both felt the ground shiver. We stood still, each one watching the face of the other one shiver. The road trembled hard beneath us, and the moment dragged open. He opened his mouth and shouted and I turned. A crowd of people moved in tandem down the centre of the street, dragging a cloud of dust. Above the cluster of crowns another head rose. I saw a metal face with a dark proboscis, pointing at me. For an instant I could see into the eye. Men began to flood the street, running from their houses. Every voice a separate clap of thunder. One man raised his narrow arm and fired a handgun at the head of the beast. The gun made a pathetic noise, like a cracker, and only then did the grinding oblong wheels gain speed, and the people walking before them disappeared. The remnants of the human shield stood back in confusion, men and women, their eyelids, cheeks, and lips monochromed by dust. And the bodies on the ground, Julie, could not have been bodies at all.

———

I transcribe for you here the conversation that I had with the other journalist late that night:

"You don't think that you could have stopped them?"

"I didn't even think of it. I only thought, how impossible. How impossible."

"Have another drink, my friend. What will you wire back to your magazine?"

"Nothing."

"You're holding your teacup with an old woman's hands. You were very fortunate to have witnessed it. Your people will want the story. You should have interviewed the other prisoners after they were abandoned. What did you do afterwards?"

"I came back here. I walked home and peeled my fruit and put it in a bowl and washed my hands and ate at my table. I sat by the window until it was dark, thinking of nothing, and then I came to you."

"It's a hot night and you're a young man. You have to turn the muscle of your heart into something as indifferent as the muscle in your arm. We are performing a service by being here. You think that these people hate us, but you're wrong. They are indifferent to us. Their eyes are so full they've gone blind. We have to tell their story."

"Why do they need us to do that?"

"They don't. It's always someone else who gains by knowing tragedy. I can take the story from you. I can tell it for you. You can haul yourself through the streets like one of them. You can let your eyes go dark. Watch the killing, come home, eat and sleep, and then speak to me. And I'll be you. I'll be the you who needs to get paid. Drink up and write a letter home. You only look like you come from here. You were always able to leave."

"Do you think of yourself as a good man?"

"Yes. I think of you that way, too. You miss your wife and you've forgotten your name. It's a kind of fever that we all go through, and that's all."

"That's all?"

———————

Good night, Julie. Far away from me you must be kneeling down upon your shadow now; the gleam of your irises is screened from the night by your hair. I can smell your skin in the palms of my hands. Float away, only love, away from the planet's strange embrace. Tread through the cumulus of dreams. May you wake with a mouth full of violets. May you drink clean water from the tap. I'll come home to kiss you in the grass again. We will never tremble apart. Julie – fear is waking without you. So turn the bed upside down and we'll make love in the curtains. I can see your arms and legs. I can see the empty plates and glasses. I can see the gnawed corn cob. I can see the patina of rust in the white porcelain sink. I can see your fragile nightgown folded on the floor. I can see your eyelashes flickering, flickering.

Faerie Tears in Piccadilly

For my good friend, Don

THE BOY HUNG ABOUT THE DOORS of the Strathmore Hotel like a draped flag: a young, male civilian in the middle of London in the final days of a war, displayed like the representative of some tiny, neutral state. Frederick passed slowly by, barely looking, as if gripped by a humbling sense of respect. Still, he snuck quick side glances, taking in juvenile blonde hair and rough, squarish features. Out in the curving street was the swirling mass of black cabs, and in the middle of the roundabout, Eros poised with his eternally arched arrow. Frederick darted a glance back. Even though the boy hadn't budged an inch, wasn't even looking up, Frederick pulled the packet of Sweet Caps from the breast pocket of his tan summer uniform and stupidly offered them from across the crowd. His calling card, Canadian cigarettes. He himself didn't smoke, but since they were sent over from home, and were half the price of those sold in London shops, he bought his allotment of four packs a week. Because it was well-known that Canadians and Americans always had lots of smokes, it was standard practice for a man in uniform to offer, almost rude not to. And even from the distance now between them, the boy lifted a hand in acknowledgement, fingers curled and waiting.

A "rent boy." The thought sent a flutter of nervousness through Frederick, making him turn back into the crowd. He'd heard the phrase several times, always in that clipped British accent. But he was sure it didn't tell half the story of some poor kid from the East End, or from some little town in the North, wandering into the city with a plaintive need that could never be met.

Frederick looked back again as he kept on his way, following the roundabout, and the flock of pigeons orbiting the dark, bronzed god. Aluminum, actually. And not Eros at all. "The naked archer is not the God of Love as so many suspect, but the representative of Christian charity, built in honour of the Earl of Shaftesbury." Frederick had learned all this from a travelogue shown the new recruits in Bournesmouth, his first home after leaving Halifax.

A fine drizzle appeared in the air. The second or third time that day, and the same weather, it seemed, since his arrival two weeks ago – fifteen days, actually, as the marked calendar on the wall of his damp bedsit told him this morning. The tiny droplets seemed too insubstantial to fall, but hung about in the air, making cold, little kisses on his eyes and cheeks. Faerie tears, Frederick thought. Another bit from the film. "The source of the Clwyd River," the BBC voice said, "is, according to legend, the tears of the Faeries who lost their lands to the farmers and miners who settled here centuries ago. If this is so," the voice added, "there ought to be a deluge in Piccadilly Circus." A few chuckles in the audience. Not many got it, but Frederick did. Another clue in his nameless search. Like that Turkish bath back in Toronto during his training. "Take a private room," he was told. "That way the pansies won't bother you." But Frederick wanted to be bothered. And his next free evening found him hurrying down to the Oak Leaf, its address marked on the tiny, folded advert torn from the *Star*. What he found there was another kind of vegetation: not open, shiny, pansy-faced versions of the bright, young faces that surrounded him daily. There was no Frank Cicconne, or "Groundspeed" McKenna – sturdy and solid – whom Frederick pictured turning to him the way the young men usually responded to the Toronto office girls on their downtown lunch hours. Instead, there were only creepy old men who attempted to attach themselves like parasitic weeds to those who stayed too long in one place.

More recently, and most daring, was Frederick's venture into Leicester Square, and down the dirty stone steps to the public lavs. There, after a long wait, standing between the short marble dividers, he'd reached out to what was offered him at the next urinal. Had he really done that? His quick shuffling away and up the stairs to the street had been an attempt to erase the event, a film shown backwards, or better, cut out from the original.

And now, here he was in Piccadilly, the centre of London (if there was a centre, it was here), following the insinuations of a snide narrating voice, leading him to doom, most likely. For in truth, Frederick was much more nervous about "getting caught" then anything else, including the war. But like the war, this nervousness, this fear, was a kind of electrical buzz that kept life charged.

Bombs dropped from the sky from time to time, and dropped on everyone indiscriminately. But the Blitz was over. And as for Hitler's new rockets – the V2's – they said the English rain confused their delicate navigating systems. One had barrelled into Kensington Square the other day, and if it had blown up like it was supposed to, it would have taken out several blocks. Instead, it appeared to morning passers-by like a kind of mysterious, gnarled sculpture work, an extravagant, crazy gift. "Arrows thrown by a dying giant," read the *Times* caption beneath a murky picture of steaming iron. But, it seemed to Frederick, Hitler's treatment of the English was more that of a drunken, loutish lover – at one time frightening, now so obviously frightened.

Not far different from himself, he thought. For Frederick, too, felt his strength drained by the loss of his own personal war. On the ship over, he'd been chosen, probably because of his build, to lug whole sides of beef up from the ship's larder to the kitchen – sometimes twice a day. It was a job he'd hated – the smell had made him more nauseous than anything the swaying sea could do to him. Still, it had gotten him more food than regular duty and had given him a hell of a workout. Anyways, he'd been told often enough in a grudging half insult, that he was "built like a brick shithouse." Now, with his new "mission" – not the aviation mechanic he'd trained to be in Toronto, not lifting and heaving heavy powerful engines and cylinders – as a processor of applications for English war brides, Frederick felt the volume of his thighs, of his shoulders, of his arms, wasted under the weight of the paper stack that was each day deposited on the corner of his desk. He watched his thick hands fingering these applications of good, clear conscience, and he pictured his own court-martial. His position of being privy to so much personal information on the lives of England's bright, young women would add an extra level of perversity and shame to his licentious charge. To top it all, he was RCAF – its membership already maligned as being *comme ça*, an epithet usually accompanied by the terrible broken wrist gesture. Frederick imagined his case trumped up as a prime example, his name mythically disseminated throughout the Army and Navy, for

33

all the generations and wars to come.

Despite all these calamitous risks, Frederick threw another glance in the direction of the hotel as he left the traffic circle west along Piccadilly. The blond head was just a tiny spot of yellow now, and yet Frederick thought he distinguished a flicker of response there. He kept walking, then turned and checked again. This time, it was gone. Ridiculous, he thought, almost mouthing the word to himself. Still looking, however, he caught sight of the figure moving, this time through the crowd and coming – Frederick was sure of it – in his direction.

Frederick turned and kept walking, all the way down Piccadilly towards the Wellington Arch, keeping a slow pace, narrowing the distance between them. In addition to this, he stopped along the way in front of shop windows, as if his interest were caught by a wide variety of things – from ladies' hats to orthopaedic shoes.

Finally Frederick reached the edge of the park, and by this time, the boy was no more than twenty feet behind. Frederick hadn't really planned at all to lure this boy or anyone back to his room. In fact, he didn't know what he'd planned. But following this path along the edge of the Serpentine was certainly part of his homeward route. Once they reached the other side of the park they would be well on their way to his door in Bayswater. If he was going to change his mind, he'd better do it now. He made another stop and looked out at the water, at the toy boats, as rare as their young owners with their nannies, the majority of whom had long ago abandoned London and its rain of bombs.

Just then, a rare patch of blue drifted in line with the forgotten sun, and the lake ignited with a million sparkling reflections. Frederick looked back at the boy. They were close enough now to determine a nervousness in the boy's posture. Not such a rent boy after all, Frederick thought. He could also make out that the boy's eyes were half closed, either from the sudden glare, or a downward glance drawn to Frederick's lower body. This last possibility had a miraculous effect on Frederick. Like sheafs of dried paper or flakes of ashes dispersed in a breeze, all of his misgivings – his ever-present, dreary fears – suddenly fell away from him. His chest expanded, and he became incredibly aware of his own body – of his chest, his shoulders, his arms, his thighs. Aware, not in the way he'd been on the ship, straining against weights of physical labour, and not the way he'd felt pressing against the wood of his desk that supported the thousands of signatures of English brides. Here, perhaps for the first time ever, he felt totally clear of all that. He was floating and expansive, a real "catch," and for the first time that day, he smiled.

By the time Frederick reached his door, his hard-on had worked its way through the fly of his air-force issue underwear – worn to a diaphanous veil by countless industrial washings – to come in contact with the rough caress of his khakis. He slowed his pace even more; in fact, all his actions turned into a kind of slow-motion film. He left the door ajar and climbed the stairs one step at a time, extending the sound of each individual creak. Finally, he was at his own doorway, looking in at his bed, unmade from the morning. He remembered his urgency to get out, the feeling that there was no time to fix anything up.

Creaks echoing his own from a moment before came up behind him. Frederick turned. Up close, the boy appeared a little smaller and a little older than what Frederick had thought. In fact, they were both about the same height and probably about the same age. The rough-hewn worker features were there, though tempered by a delicacy, brought about by a lifetime of bad nutrition and want. Once again, Frederick pulled out his cigarettes. "Ta, mate," the boy said, the first sound he'd made – more a timorous bray or bird's clipped song than a voice. His fingers, lifting to accept the gift, grazed the bulge in Frederick's trousers, an acceptable accident. Frederick responded by pulling off his own jacket, letting it drop to the floor. The boy smiled, the cigarette now between his lips.

Thinking back afterwards, Frederick couldn't quite believe that the bomb went off just as he lit the match. The two of them dropped to the floor as if struck, though nothing struck them. It was just the sound of an incredible blast high above. Another V2 rocket, as Frederick would later find out, exploded above Hyde Park, shaking the surrounding city blocks, shattering a few windows, but doing no real damage.

They both slowly rose and looked out the window. The sky was an incredible blue now, as if the blast had cleared out all of London's clouds. Clear, but for a great ring of smoke floating over the trees of the park, as if left there by a giant. Accompanying the cloud was a symphony of approaching sirens, getting louder and louder. All the buildings in the "affected zone," Frederick knew, would be checked out. He looked around the room and imagined how it would appear: the unmade bed, his RCAF jacket strewn on the floor and, of course, his visitor standing near him, trembling and scared. Frederick reached out an arm and held him close.

A Working Dyke's Dream

KAREN X. TULCHINSKY

WHEN I FIRST STARTED WORKING at Gulliver's Travel, my boss was a balding, middle-aged man named Seymour Plotkin. Two months ago, he had a nervous breakdown after his wife ran off with their gardener. For a week I didn't have a boss. The following Monday I was sitting at my computer when the front door opened. I heard footsteps approaching and looked up to find a beautiful woman standing in front of my desk. She was smiling right at me. I smiled back as she stuck out her hand.

"Hi," she said, "I'm Sadie Singer, the new manager."

I knew I was supposed to stand up, shake her hand, introduce myself, show her around, all that normal stuff, but I couldn't take my eyes off her soft full lips, her finely sculpted cheekbones or her big brown eyes that melted right through my Monday morning haze. With gargantuan effort, I raised my hand and took hers, desperately forcing myself to give her a businesslike handshake, when really I felt like raising her hand to my lips and planting a tender kiss on her smooth olive skin. My knees were shaking as I pushed my steno chair backward and stood up. I was just a little taller than she was. My eyes met hers. She was a goddess. A short, voluptuous, brown-eyed, frizzy-haired movie star. She walked right off the pages of *People* magazine and into Gulliver's Travel. She was too glamorous to be in the travel business. I must be on *Candid Camera*, I thought. I looked around for Allen Funt.

"You must be Barbara," she said in a deep, husky ex-smoker's voice.

"Please," I begged, "call me Bobby. Everyone does."

She held onto my hand a beat longer than necessary.

"All right ... Bobby." She smiled and dropped my hand. It

plunged back down to earth and hung limply at my side, my fingers vibrating from her touch. I stared into her eyes, silently thanking whatever higher power had caused Mr. Plotkin's wife to run off with a younger man so that I could be blessed with a boss like Sadie Singer. A working dyke's dream. A boss who looks like Bette Midler, Madonna, Jessica Lange, and Queen Latifah all rolled into one. Instead of answering "Yes, sir" to a fat, middle-aged man, I would now be working with a Hollywood bombshell.

"Bobby, why don't you show me around? Then I'd like to start in on organizing my office. I understand Mr. Plotkin left in a hurry and that things are in some disarray."

Please, allow me to show you the inside of the supply cupboard, or better yet, my apartment, I wanted to say. "There's not much to show," I said instead. "We're pretty small. Just me, Jack – he's off sick today – and Jerry over there." I pointed to my co-worker, a flamboyant old drag queen who dressed as butch as he could during the day so he could make a living in the business world. Even then, he looked like Diana Ross in a three-piece suit, or like an older, darker Michael Jackson before his last two nose jobs. Butch and femme both at the same time.

I led the way to the back of the storefront office so I could introduce Sadie to Jerry. She followed behind me so closely I could almost feel her nipples pressing against my back. It was growing warmer inside the office and I reached up and undid the top button of my shirt.

As we approached, Jerry stood, stuck out his hand and half curtsied. "Well, at least you're a better dresser than poor old Mr. Plotkin. No wonder his wife left him."

"Thank you, Jerry," Sadie laughed. "I'll take that as a compliment."

I led my new boss over to the lunchroom, which had a small fridge, a coffee machine, and a table and chairs. At the very back was an oversize closet that we called the supply room. Inside, I began pointing out the elaborate inventory system that Mr. Plotkin had set up. There were stacks of vacation brochures, corporate flight planners, and travel-insurance folders to show her. I had my back to Sadie as I opened drawers and cupboards to let her see inside. When I turned around I saw that her eyes were all over my body. For a moment I didn't know if she was straight or gay or what. I could feel a fine sweat forming on my skin, and I casually rolled my shirt sleeves up to my elbows. I spent a long time explaining where we ordered the Xerox paper from, while in my mind I could see myself leaning her up against the shelves and opening her buttons slowly, one by one, until her magnificent breasts leaped out at me. Silently, she would guide my hand underneath her skirt and I would feel her wetness calling me up inside of her, and there, in the closet, I would plunge my fingers into her, and she would urge me on and on, until she was coming and calling out my name. Her back would be indented by the stacks of Club Med brochures, but she wouldn't care. She'd lean back after and have a cigarette and maybe give me a raise and invite me home to dinner.

"Fine." Her voice came out of nowhere, bringing me back from my fantasy. "I think we've covered the supply room quite sufficiently."

"Right," I agreed, wiping the sweat from my forehead with the back of my hand.

Somehow I made it back to my desk without laying a hand on her. She went into her glass-enclosed office and began going through the files. From where I sat I had a clear view of her. Whenever she'd reach for a manila folder on her desk, she had to bend slightly, teasing me with the sight of her ample cleavage. Every so often she'd glance in my direction and I was sure she was checking me out, too. I pretended to type words on my keyboard. I shuffled papers from one side of my desk to the other, but all the while I had one eye on Sadie and the other turned inward to watch the scores of fantasies being projected inside my head. All that morning, I was a one-woman porno production company. If I could have captured the images on film, I'd have made a fortune in the X-rated movie business.

At noon, I still had one eye on Sadie as she casually freshened her lipstick. With all the care she was taking with her appearance, I knew she must be meeting someone. I pretended to be concentrating deeply on the Air Canada flight information on my monitor as she walked past me, saying she'd be back at one o'clock.

"You bet," I grinned. "See you then." I watched her walk by my desk. She couldn't see me now, so I took the opportunity to devour her from behind. She was so femme I almost died at the sight of her. I could have sworn she was wearing those old-fashioned stockings with the seam up the back. Her perfume wafted into my nose and I swooned, breathing deeply her womanly scent. Her ass was perfect, just how derrieres were meant to be – round, full, and big. It bounced and danced from side to side as she sauntered out the front glass door and into the street. I felt like a teenage boy in the fifties who had just gotten his first glimpse of Marilyn Monroe. My heart was racing, my palms sweating, my eyes singing a hundred rhapsodies to her. The second she was gone, I switched off my screen, grabbed my jacket, and yelled back to Jerry. "See you at one. Out for lunch."

Before I knew exactly what I was doing, I was outside on Georgia Street. It was an unusually brilliant winter day. Snow glistened on the peaks of the North Shore mountains. Ahead of me I could see Sadie. She was walking briskly, heading south, down Burrard Street. It took another few blocks before I realized I was following her. I stayed close to the wall so that, in case she turned around, I could duck into the nearest shop or office building. I didn't want her to see me, but I knew I wanted to see who she was meeting. Woman or man? Husband? Lover? Friend? I needed to know if she was straight or gay or what. I didn't stop to think about how ridiculous I was being. There was no time for that. I didn't want to lose her.

At the Sky-Train station, she took the escalator down to the mall under the big office towers. It was a typical Vancouver fast-food fair, with pizza and Chinese food and sushi and espresso and falafel stands all around the perimeter, and hundreds of orange tables with yellow plastic chairs attached to them in the middle. Between noon and one on a weekday, the place was packed. Perfect. I could find a seat far enough away to be hidden, yet close enough to see what Sadie was up to. Keeping a respectable distance, I followed her down into the mall. For a moment I almost lost her, so I hurried forward, pushing people out of my way to get ahead.

At the bottom of the escalator I shoved a man a little too hard, knocking his phone from his grasp and into the air where it did a little cellular flip.

"Hey!" the man shouted. People all around us turned and stared, including Sadie, who stood a few feet away against a wall. Standing beside her was a tall, thin, suit-wearing, short-haired woman who was a dyke for sure and a butch to boot. I gawked, feeling the blood rise in my cheeks. Sadie's eyes were locked on mine. Foolishly, I gripped the escalator handrail for support. It rolled around on its track and pulled me down with it. My eyes were jerked away from

40

hers by the force, and I heard Sadie start to giggle. By the time I struggled back to my feet, all I could see was her beautiful feminine back as she and her butch disappeared into the lunch-crowd abyss. I clapped my hands together in joy, because her lunchtime companion confirmed my suspicions that Sadie was a member of the club. A friend of Dorothy's. A graduate of the Isle of Lesbos. A certified, card-carrying homo. Or at the very least, bisexual, and therefore erotically interested in women, and specifically butch women, which at the time was all I needed to know. I smiled all the way back to the office.

When Sadie came back from lunch I did not look up. I was furiously poring over flight schedules on my computer. I could smell her perfume and knew she was standing right in front of my desk.

"You shouldn't spy on people," she said. "It's not nice. Besides, it's dangerous. You might find out something you're not supposed to know." I looked up with one eye closed, as if I was scared she would hit me or something. I saw that she was half-smirking as she turned on her heels and swished toward her glass-enclosed, semiprivate office. I guess I should have been embarrassed. Strangely, I was not. I felt light, even happy.

The next Monday Sadie was later than usual getting into work. At ten o'clock the front door swung open and she stomped past my desk, marched into her office, and slammed the door. All morning long, she paced. She opened drawers and banged them shut, crumpled pieces of paper into tight little balls and shot them into the garbage can across the room. For part of the morning, she sat at her desk quietly staring into space. I decided she must have had a fight with her lover. Her mood had all the markings of marital hell. I figured it was best to just stay out of her way.

At five o'clock, Jerry and Jack said goodbye for the day, but I was behind in my paperwork, so I decided to work late to catch up. I was deeply engrossed in my computer screen when I smelled Sadie's perfume drifting toward me. I looked up when she was standing right above me.

"I want you, Bobby," she said, her deep brown eyes penetrating mine.

"What?" I was in shock.

"You heard me."

I turned off my screen. "Now?"

"Now."

"Here?"

She looked around, grabbed my hand, and dragged me toward the lunch area. "Here," she said as she pulled me inside the supply room and locked the door.

As much as I had been waiting, dreaming, hoping, and praying for this moment, I needed to know why. I stepped back. "What's going on?" I asked her.

She sighed deeply and leaned against stacks of "Experience Alaska" brochures. "My lover has been cheating on me," she spit icily. "I finally found out. All our friends know. I'm the last to find out. Why are lovers always the last to know?"

"I don't know."

"Anyway, who cares?" She held out her hand. "Come here, Bobby."

I paused for a moment. She looked so beautiful in her grief and her pain and her passion. I wanted her more than ever, and I could see that she wanted me, but for all the wrong reasons. She wanted to use me to get back at her cheating girlfriend. I could have been anybody. As for me – I'd be a homewrecker, the other woman. I'd be corrupting the morals of a married woman. I looked back at her and I knew I didn't care. She wanted me and that's all that mattered. Ever since she walked into Gulliver's Travel and into my life, with that gorgeous body and all her femme charm, I knew that this moment would come.

I saw her outstretched hand and I took it. She pulled me to her and I went. I raised my free hand to her beautiful, angry face and I kissed her. My passion was an ancient volcano. Lava had been building up for hundreds of years inside my aching body. My desire for her was immense. I poured every ounce of its greatness into that first kiss. It was a kiss to die for, deep and wet and explosive. She pulled away and looked at me, trying to catch her breath. I waited to see what she would do. She licked her lips provocatively. Then she flung herself back into my arms, her mouth on mine, hard, urgent and wanting. We kissed again and I wrapped my arms around her, pulling her toward me, desperate to touch her all over. I wanted to see her naked. From the beginning I'd been watching her, undressing her with my eyes, wondering how her body would feel next to mine. I pulled back from her and slowly began to undo the tiny buttons on her purple silk blouse. She rested her hands lightly on my waist and watched. The smooth material slid down her arms easily. I caught the shirt as it fell and carefully hung it on the corner of a shelf. Then I stepped back a few inches so I could see her better. Her soft round breasts spilled out over the top of her black lacy bra.

"Feel them," she said. "I know you want to."

I raised my hands and held her breasts, feeling the weight of them, feeling her nipples grow hard. She reached behind and undid the clasp. The elastic loosened and her bra fell into my hands. I couldn't contain myself any longer. I moved in and buried my face in her fullness. She ran her fingers through my hair and then down my back.

"Take off your shirt," she ordered.

I pulled back again as I tore at my buttons and ripped off my shirt, letting it fall to the floor near my feet. I wrapped my arms around her waist, pulling her into me tightly. My hands were around her ass. She was half-sitting on my thigh. I could feel her heat right through her skirt. She was warm and wet and ready for me. I reached for her tenderly and slipped my hands under the waistband of her panties. She spread her legs apart, and I moved my hand to her slippery cunt. She moaned and forced herself onto my eager fingers, and then I remembered. I pulled out. She looked up at me with big, questioning eyes.

"What's wrong, Bobby?"

"Shit!" I said. "God, I miss the seventies."

"What?!"

"Safe sex. You know. We need latex gloves or a dental dam, a condom, anything."

"Oh, God." Her desire for me was palpable. There had to be something we could do. I pulled free of her and looked around, leaving her leaning against the shelves, out of breath and longing. I staggered into the lunchroom, searching for something, anything that even resembled a latex glove. Desperately, I looked in the fridge. The answer was staring me in the face. On the bottom rack my uneaten cheese sandwich from the day before still sat in a clear plastic bag. I laughed and lunged for it. The sandwich slipped out and I tossed it into the garbage. I went back to her, holding up my prize. She giggled as I shook out the crumbs and slid my hand into the baggie.

"Oh, Bobby, don't make me wait any longer," she hissed, and I was back in her arms, my gloved hand up her dress and inside her underwear. Urgently I felt for her opening and slid one finger in. She grabbed for me with her cunt and I gave her another finger and then another. She was moving on me like her life depended on it. In all my twenty-seven years of living I had never been with such a wild woman. The world slipped away from us. We were nothing but a hand and a cunt, and she tore at the flesh on my back with her nails, crying, "Yes, baby, yes, I want you to fuck me, don't stop." And I gave her all that I had to give, and she took it and took it until she was coming. Deep, heaving waves of muscles contracting on my fingers.

44

"Oh, Sadie. You're beautiful," I whispered in her ear, and I meant every word. I was so happy I thought I would burst.

Then I held her as her breathing calmed and she clutched me, her body tight against mine. We were sweating right onto a pile of "Adventures in Beautiful B.C." pamphlets. My hand was still inside of her. I think we were in love, just for that moment. She was still my boss. She still had a lover who cheated on her. But in that instant we were the two happiest dykes the world had ever known. I wanted it to go on forever.

I knew that soon she would pull away, adjust her clothes, and we would both go home. She to her lover. Me to my empty apartment. We would not fall in love. She would not leave her lover for me. She would still be my boss. And I would keep on searching for the woman of my dreams. And yet, each Monday morning, when I drag myself reluctantly into work for the start of another long week, I know I'll always have Sadie, the beautiful voluptuous boss lady, across the room to daydream about. I'll never forget the feel of her cunt on my hand, the softness of her breasts against mine or her powerful, womanly scent.

I reached up and stroked her hair, and we stayed like that for a long time. Then I brought my lips to hers and we kissed. I felt her body moving just a little, her passion building again. I smiled because I knew that the great romantics would always have Paris, Bogart and Bergman would always have Casablanca, and for the rest of our lives, Sadie and I would always have Gulliver's Travel.

Night Train

NELL CARBERRY

WELL, I'D SAY WE WERE DRUNK except that neither of us drinks, but we'd drunk enough lattés to send us into the next galaxy. My skin was tingling, and Joe kept picking up my hand and dropping it, each time dragging a finger across my palm.

He was young and tattooed and shaved and pierced, and I was about ten years older. "Vanilla skin," he called me. But he wouldn't tell me his last name, or what he did, so I told him, no way would I take him home with me. I was that kind of girl, but I wasn't *that* kind of girl.

"So let me ride the train home with you, at least, " he said. "Let me make you feel safe."

I didn't feel safe around him. He had pale skin and deep blue eyes, and the slightest hint of a brogue. The tattoos were mostly Celtic designs, and his pale scalp stubble hinted that when it grew, he had dark air. Black Irish, I thought.

It was 2AM on a Sunday night, and we boarded the train at Broadway-Lafayette. Both dressed for city combat: white t-shirts, black jeans, heavy boots.

And we entered an empty car, empty but for the trash blowing around.

And as we approached a seat, he said, "So you won't fuck me at your place, Nell?"

"Not without further particulars," I replied.

At this point we were kissing and sucking each other's fingers, sticky with the coffee we'd downed. We'd both been bad drinkers once, but now coffee and sex were the drugs of choice.

"Not in your house," he said again, and grabbed my shoulders from behind, licked my neck. I would have told him anything right then, but then he quickly slid his hands down my arms and grabbed my wrists. He pulled my arms overhead, and kept both wrists trapped in one meaty hand.

With the other, he pulled out a set of handcuffs. They jangled so loud. Just at that point, the doors flew open. Last stop in Manhattan.

"You can get off now, if you'd like," Joe said, and loosened the pressure on my hands just a bit.

But I shook my head. Let's see where this goes, I thought.

"You could take me home to your bed," he hissed, and shook the handcuffs.

"No," I said, and Joe flipped open the cuffs and slammed them on my wrists, carefully suspending me from the overhead pole. I was still facing away from him, but I could see everything he was doing in the smudged subway window. My feet barely touched the floor.

We were underground, in a tunnel beneath the East River.

"I'm not a bad man," Joe explained. "I just don't like to be denied."

Then he yanked my shirt up and exposed my bra, shoving a hand into the soft, sweaty cotton. He came around so he was facing me and pulled my breast to his mouth. The cuffs hurt my wrists, but they seemed to build the sensation in my nipple. I was moaning. Joe was silent. His tongue was long and pink, and I could smell smoke on his skin. He lapped at my breast like a baby. His jeans bulged. I tried to move closer, get more of his mouth on my tit, but he backed away. And again, he moved behind me.

First stop in Brooklyn, York Street, the ghost town stop. Still, I looked over my shoulder to see if anyone was entering. For a moment, I had a flash that Joe would make whoever enter the car join our handcuff party. I felt ashamed. And very hot.

"I get off in six stops," I said, suddenly angry.

"Oh, you do, do you," Joe said, impishly. "Then we'll have to hurry this along."

Joe unbuttoned my jeans and yanked them to the floor, where they lay in a heap around my feet. I felt doubly trapped, a cloth bond around my legs, a metal one around my wrists. I was still wearing underwear, stupid white cotton briefs, because while I always wanted sex, I never believed I'd get it on the first date.

"Practical panties," Joe said, and ground himself into my back. I could feel his erection looking for a place to rest, and as he slid around my ass, it fit perfectly in my ass crack. I could hear Joe unzip and in the window I saw his cock rise in the air, bobbing. Sweat dripped off his face and onto my back. I heard him reach in a back pocket, and that familiar metallic sound, ripping, stretching.

"Next time," he growled, as he rolled it over his cock, "you'll put it on with your mouth."

"What makes you think there'll be a next time?" I snapped. Then he spanked me once, and I moaned.

"Don't pretend with me, Nell."

And then he stuck his hand in my panties and ripped them off. They fell in a heap, too. And before I could object, he had one hand dithering my clit, the other stroking my ass crack.

"You really have to get home?" he murmured into my hair.

"No!" I moaned. "I mean, yes."

"All right," he sighed. Then he grabbed my breasts and plunged his cock deep into me.

Suddenly we were one with the train's rhythm, just as it rose above the ground, into the sparkling Brooklyn sky. His cock was the right size for me, and he kept hitting my g-spot like he had a map. When I tried to back into *him*, he would hold me still.

"You are my little fuckdoll tonight, Nell," he said, and then two stops from my destination, he pounded at me in earnest, fingering my clit all the way. The only sounds: the train, moans, the unmistakable sound of precome mixing with latex. And because of the way we were positioned, we could see ourselves fucking in the window.

As could anyone who was in the station. A few sleepy partiers gaped at the next stop, but they didn't get in. One man actually did a double take: a rarity in New York.

And all the while, the heat was rising in me, and Joe's cock was pulsing. His hands pinched my nipples, as if trying to pull the orgasm out of me.

"I feel so embarrassed," I said.

"No ... you ... don't," said Joe, pumping with each word for emphasis. "No. You. Don't."

Now Joe was groaning, and he was very close. His hand drifted to my face, and I nipped his fingers with my mouth, drawing them in, sucking them, and he came closer. One and a half stops to my destination.

"You're my fuckdoll, and you'll do anything I tell you," said Joe. "Tell me what you are."

47

"I'm your fuckdoll and I'll do anything you say."

"No, I said, 'anything I *tell* you.'"

I was quiet.

"Say the words right, or I'll pull out and leave you in the train."

Words were just words, I thought. And I needed that orgasm. Still....

Then he said it.

"Nell, please."

So he needed it, too.

"I'm your fuckdoll," I said slowly, and Joe pumped me with every word, and I was seconds from going over the edge.

"... and I'll do anything you tell me."

And then we came together, bent, standing, convulsing, seeing ourselves in the glass, panting, coming some more. As soon as we stopped quivering, Joe moved quickly to unchain me and zip himself up. My arms ached, my mouth was dry, and I could have done it the rest of the night.

Joe yanked my pants up and picked up my ripped panties from the floor.

"Joe needs Fuckdoll's number," he said in a sweet pleading voice, and so I wrote it, quickly, on the soiled and sweaty cotton. It didn't occur to me to do otherwise.

The doors of the subway train parted, and we kissed, Joe nipping my mouth, just a little.

He grabbed me by the shoulders and propelled me out of the train.

"You gave me what I wanted, now I'll give you what you really want," Joe said. I turned to face him.

"My last name's O'Riley," he smirked. Then the doors closed again. And he was gone.

Autobiography of a Tattoo (2: The Barracks)

STAN PERSKY

IN THE SAN DIEGO U.S. NAVY BOOT CAMP BARRACKS one night shortly after lights out, one of the four of us (not me) suggested that we jack-off to see if the chemical (saltpeter) that was allegedly put into our food to reduce our sexual urges really worked.

We happened to be billeted at the end of the barracks, afforded some privacy by a wall of lockers, in two double-bunk beds, slim Donnie from New Mexico above me, and in the next double-bunk over, beefy Bruehl from Arizona on top, and in the lower bunk, a boy from somewhere in the South, curiously named Richard Richards. Although he tried to get us to pronounce his surname "Reichart," we simply dropped the "s" on his last name and subjected him to the accusation that his hillbilly parents were so dumb that they couldn't think up another first name for him. "Richard, on the double!" the company commander or drill sergeant would call out. "That's Reichart, sir," he would plead, in a doomed effort at correction.

Name-play was crucial in the ongoing daily struggle over the barracks pecking order. My own name was easily elided from Persky to Pesky to Pussky to Pussy, and to be a "pussy," i.e., a girl, was tantamount to social death. As if to confirm it, I was relatively inept at accomplishing the tasks that constituted our training, and yet, the distinctions made were fine-grained enough that I was nonetheless considered a real, if mediocre, guy, and spared the contempt of being consigned to the category of the lowest-of-the-low, occupied by a whiny, uncharmingly awkward kid named Gorney – who was instantly dubbed "Horny Gorney" – and who was eventually actually dumped, head-first, into the barracks' metal garbage can. Whereas I, for all my failings (unable to swim, not very good with guns, etc.), managed to elicit the sympathetic attention of one of the barracks' tough guys, a kid named Harsh, also from Arizona, who invited me one day to do some practice wrestling with him, thus publicly demonstrating that I wasn't to be considered a complete wimp.

The companies were assembled in random fashion, on the basis of the coincidental arrival of busloads of recruits from various parts of the country. We were a group of Midwesterners, bused out to the Coast from the Great Lakes Naval Training Station near Chicago; a gangly, giraffe-like, but prematurely sober guy from Milwaukee named Brinkhoff was named our recruit company commander, a position he retained once the whole company was put together. (I remember him offering me some "buck-up, kid" fatherly consolation once when I was feeling homesick.) We arrived in the middle of the night, were issued blankets and some other gear, and bundled off to the barracks.

The next morning, on the "grinder," a vast, asphalt-paved, sun-fried marching area in the centre of the San Diego boot camp, we sleepily met our company-mates, a group of boys from the American Southwest, mainly Arizona, and were marched off in raggedy order to the mess hall. I'm not sure how Richards (or Reichart) got to be with us; maybe he was from Tennessee or Kentucky and got lumped in with the Midwesterners.

In the semi-darkness, perhaps illuminated by some stray moonlight pouring in from a nearby window, we reached into our underwear (there was a Navy word for them, what was it? – now I remember: "skivvies"!) or maybe pulled our skivvies down to mid-thigh, and began to masturbate. Although it didn't occur to me at the time, the proposal (whoever made it) had the function of alleviating our embarrassment about the problem of secretly jacking off. To the sounds of the gentle ship-like creaking of the metal double-bunks and our own increasingly excited breathing, we entered eternity. I came easily.

Then there occurred the moment that further changed my life forever. While Bruehl and Donnie were privately occupied above, Reichart – though we refused to call him that, as he wanted, I always thought of him as Reichart – whispered to me from his bunk. In memory, our bunks are shoved closer together – only inches apart – than they could have been in actuality. I can't remember his precise words, though from time to time I'm still able to see him in memory, not so much beautiful as sexy, freckles across the bridge of his snub nose, skinny hips. It went something like, "Hey, I can only get it up half-way," and then he asked me to help him, to jack him off a little with my own hand. I refused. "Aw, come on," he said in his sly, cajoling, half-promising, persuasive way that no one in their right mind could refuse.

Or at least I couldn't. I reached out from my bunk to his. His hand took mine and placed it around his velvety but hard cock. I remember feeling, just before being overwhelmed by other emotions, an instant of confusion – he had claimed to be only semi-erect, but his cock in fact felt pretty hard to me – innocently unaware that his small fib was in service to his seduction of me.

Guiding my hand with his own, Reichart moved it up and down the sheath of his foreskin, instructing me in the motion he liked, hoping that once I learned the movement I would continue it on my own. I was in ecstasy, terrified ecstasy, ecstatic terror. But instead of continuing to masturbate him, I withdrew my hand. He tried to coax me. I wasn't to be persuaded.

He would have his revenge the next day, saying to the guys at our table in the mess hall – to Bruehl and Donnie immediately, but others were also within hearing, "Hey, you know what Pussy did to me last night when we were jacking off? He played with my dick," thus, not only confirming my lowly status as a pussy, but raising the prospect that I was also a "fruit." Naturally, I furiously, but carefully – not wanting to excite further suspicion by protesting too much – denied Reichart's charge.

Meanwhile, above us, in their respective bunks, oblivious to the whispered drama below, Bruehl and Donnie carried on. Shortly after I'd come, Donnie triumphantly declared, "I came!" He was a teenager with fine, delicately-shaped facial features, almost feminine in his beauty, and had, by way of self-protection I suppose, developed a slightly nasty, pugnacious edge to his personality. "I don't believe you, you're shitting us," Bruehl said. "Here," Donnie replied to the challenge, stretching out his cupped hand containing his come in the direction of Bruehl's nose. Bruehl took a whiff. "Pee-uuu!" Bruehl reported, confirming Donnie's success. At which point, memory breaks down, dissolves, but that's not at all the end.

First, what if I hadn't refused Reichart? What if I'd continued, on my own, to slide his foreskin up and down the column of his dick? What if I'd brought him off, his come running over my hand as he unclenched his thigh muscles and sighed in contentment, would he have then told the others at "chow" the next morning? Or would he have kept it a secret, using the secret to get me to do it again (and again), whenever he wanted? Would he have kept me for himself?

I had another scenario, which preserved the original scene. Reichart tells the others, and they begin mildly teasing me. I get him aside and urgently appeal to him, "You've gotta stop telling them I touched your dick, you're going to get me in trouble." As he smiles that lazy smile of his, I make my proposal: "Look, if you tell them you were just kidding, I'll jack you off." He knows he has me, but sizes me up with his shrewd, narrowed, farmboy eyes. "How do I know you will?" I look around hastily, see that there's no one to see us and, taking a chance, grab his dick through his denim workpants ("dungarees," they were called), and then rub and fondle it just long enough to convince him. "You better not chicken out," he warns me.

But he promptly brings off his end of the bargain. We're at lunch in the mess hall, and one of the other guys, maybe Bruehl, is ribbing me. "Pussy, did you really play with Richard's dick? Did you?" At which point, just as it's about to get nasty, Reichart intervenes, in a slow half-drawl, "Boy, you-all sure are hicks. You didn't believe all that stuff, did you?" And now the spotlight shifts to Reichart, chuckling and ducking his head as Bruehl tries to whack him with his sailor's boater. "You dumb shithead!" Bruehl grumbles, as Reichart sends me a telling glance.

That night, Reichart's on guard duty, and I make my way out of the barracks to the little shack outside of which he's standing watch, passing through the concrete area where we do our wash, and where clotheslines are strung up, on which we hang our sheets and cambray shirts and dungarees. In the night, the whites move slightly in the breeze, like sails, strangely glowing. "It's me," I say, before he ritually asks, "Who goes there?" "Hey," he says, pretending to be a little pleasantly surprised. "I said I would, didn't I?" I say, mock-offended that he might've doubted my word.

Inside the dark shack – we know when the patrols come by to check that the watch isn't asleep, so we're safe for a time – I unfasten the buckle of his Navy-issue cloth belt, undo his fly, and take his skivvy-covered cock in my hand, and then reach into his underpants and hold it directly, intentionally, consciously, impressed by the heat of its flesh, and his body involuntarily leans against, into mine, and I put an arm around his waist as I jack him off.

There's an elaboration of my fantasy of his seduction of me. His dungarees and skivvies are down around his ankles, and as I lean over, my shoulder against his flat belly, jacking him off with my hand, Reichart suggests, gently touching the back of my neck, "Why don't you put it in your mouth?" "No," I refuse. "Aw come on, just a little. You know you wanna," he drawls. It's the last sentence – "You know you wanna" – his making explicit his knowing of my knowing, that's the clincher.

Now I make my counter-offer: "I will if you'll jack me off." "Sure," he agrees, increasing the pressure on the back of my neck. "How do I know you will?" I ask, lifting my head up to look into his blue eyes. "What if I do it and you just go and tell the others I sucked you off?" Without hesitation, he reaches into my pants, takes hold of my already-hard cock and jacks me off enough to prove to me that if he said anything to the others about what we're doing, I'd be able to tell on him, too. "Just put it in your mouth," he urges, continuing to hold my cock and returning his other hand to the back of my neck. I slowly bend my head toward his erection, looking at it with awe as my lips get closer to its tip.

This fantasy operation proceeds in stages. Now he's playing with my butt, wants to fuck me, offers to suck my dick if I let him, etc.

Reichart knows everything about sex; we urban kids were astonished to learn that Southern farmboys regularly fucked barnyard animals; they casually assured us that fucking a cow's ass or a lanolin-smooth sheep's vagina was "the next best thing." When our marching instructors ordered us to close our ranks to "cornhole distance," they knew all about shoving corncobs up asses. Apparently that was a favoured farm product for anal stimulation – in fact, I once saw an ear of corn so used in a porno flick about French rural life. Eventually, "cornholing" became a general term referring to anal intercourse. And in assembly and marching terminology, "cornhole distance" jokingly meant close enough to fuck the guy in front of you.

In one version, in which Reichart now has me trained and admitting that I like it, he turns up one night with Donnie in tow, generously prepared to share me with his mates.

In this masturbatory scenario played over so many times, persistent for so long, fantasy has come to seem almost indistinguishable from memory; the importance of distinguishing the two seems increasingly less important. Though I have a memory, I've little sense of it being a memory of myself. If Reichart, Bruehl, and

53

Donnie are still alive (now men in late middle-age – married, divorced, fathers, failures, successes), they've most likely completely forgotten that trivial, boyish incident. I once imagined or dreamed about Reichart in his late twenties, living in a trailer park with his wife and a kid, maybe talking up the waitress at the coffee shop in town where his work crew take their breaks.

Though the boy I was, aflame with desire, seems like someone else, nonetheless, his adolescent passion continues to influence me: shapes my pleasures, circumscribes my sorrows, beckons me on. I think: So that's what I'm left with; or more accurately, that's what I've been given; that's what I've got.

Seeing Stars

MARCY SHEINER

ONE OF MY FAVOURITE TURN-ONS is to be mercilessly teased, with gratification delayed for hours, even days. And one of my favorite ways of being teased is for a man to fondle and caress me while he remains cool and detached. Far from this being some form of masochism, when a man stays firmly in control, I feel a sense of security that allows me to abandon all self-restraint. When my partner's foot is on the brakes, I can step on the gas. With that kind of solidity to ground me, I invariably turn into a raving nymphomaniac.

I was reminded of where my fondness for this kind of thing originated when George, my college sweetheart, called me; I hadn't heard from him in nearly five years. He told me that he and his wife had just taken their daughter to a planetarium for the first time, and as soon as the lights went out, he thought about me.

I chuckled at the mere mention of the word *planetarium*.

"Remember?" George asked, chuckling himself.

"Do I remember? George, I still fantasize about that day."

"I have never seen a woman, before or since, get that hot," George told me.

We chatted about our spouses, our kids, our work. As we said goodbye, George sang softly, "I'll see you in the stars above."

I laughed. "Bye, George."

"So long, babe." My heart nearly cracked. George was the first man to ever call me "babe" and the sound of the word used to melt my insides.

It's not that I don't have a satisfying sex life; in fact, my husband Don and I have managed to keep our bedroom relationship fresh and creative for nearly eleven years. We make sure we take time for ourselves away from the kids. We indulge each other's fantasies, play silly games, even dress up in costumes occasionally. Still, when I hung up the phone I felt a sad, sweet nostalgia for my first love. I closed my eyes and allowed my thoughts to take me back to a more innocent, youthful time in my life.

George was my first lover; I was his third. We were freshmen at the University of Chicago, and after three months of dating, we started sleeping together. The discovery of my body's erotic capabilities opened up a whole new world for me, a world I wanted to explore almost constantly. I clawed at George's body at every opportunity, urging him to penetrate my mouth or pussy. Naturally, George, a young, red-blooded American college boy, was happy to oblige – but his favourite thing was to tease me. He would pretend to be disinterested, all the while doing little things to keep me in a feverish state. He loved to watch me go wild while he maintained an outwardly cool demeanour – and he especially liked to see me out of control in public places where our passion could not possibly be consummated.

One Saturday afternoon we decided to catch the sky show at Chicago's planetarium. We'd just made love that morning, but instead of feeling satisfied, I wanted more. That's how it was for me with George – making love only induced me to want more.

We sat together in the round theatre, surrounded by families on weekend outings. As soon as the lights went out, George reached over, slipped his hand underneath my blouse, and rubbed my nipple with his thumb in a slow, steady movement. His gaze was directed not at me, but at the domed ceiling covered with simulated stars and planets. I looked at his face – he was completely absorbed in the sky show, seemingly oblivious to the effect he was having on me with his thumb's methodical movements.

This one little gesture turned me on more than the most energetic of bedroom acrobatics, and my pussy dripped all over my panties. I squirmed in my seat, subtly directing George's hand to my crotch. He slipped it beneath my panties and touched my burning clit, which responded as if to an electrical charge. I writhed around, manoeuvering myself so that George's hand would find its way into my cunt.

Meanwhile, the sky show went on, and George watched it with eyes unclouded by any indication of lust or passion. I was creaming all over his hand, turning into a hot puddle on the blue upholstered seat, while he remained detached. George was a clever guy for one so young. He knew that we always want what we can't have. His seeming unattainability made me want him more, and his lack of emotional display drove me wild.

I turned sideways so I could kiss and suck on his neck and ears. My hand groped around his crotch. His face may have been inexpressive, but the hardness I found in his pants betrayed his desire. I fumbled with his zipper.

"Control yourself," he admonished, slapping my hand away as if he were swatting at an insect. I moaned.

"Let me touch it," I begged.

"Behave yourself," he scolded, cruelly withdrawing his hand from underneath my panties. A cold gush of air filled the space his hand had warmed.

I sat there feeling dizzy, every molecule in my body rioting, as lights flashed across the domed ceiling and children oohed and ahhed in appreciation of the sky show. In a few minutes, George's fingers snaked their way into my lap once more, and I gratefully pushed my groin against them. I flung a leg over one of his and humped his thigh. He pushed me away, but continued to flick his fingers over my engorged clit while he laughed with the rest of the audience at some feeble joke told by the emcee.

I had no idea what the joke or the show was about, or who was around us. Nor did I care. All my attention was focussed on one goal – getting into George's pants. Quick as lightning, I unzipped his fly, pulled out his throbbing member and dropped to the floor, swiftly taking him into my mouth. George put his big hands on either side of my head and, after a mighty struggle, managed to pry me loose. He shoved me back into my chair, zipped up his pants and moved a few seats away from me. In a panic I followed him.

"George," I hissed, "don't do this to me." A few heads turned in our direction.

"Stop it," he said. "You're making a scene."

"But I need you. Please, if you won't do it here, let's go back to the dorm."

Again I made a grab for the bulge beneath his jeans; this time his slap on my hand was audible. More and more people were becoming aware of a disturbance, and several told us to shut up. George apologized, implying that I was some sort of madwoman. Finally, the usher came over and told us that if we didn't settle down we'd have to leave.

For the rest of the program I remained perfectly still and silent, while George audaciously resumed flicking his fingers across my nipple. Though I burned with intense desire, I knew I'd better keep a lid on it.

When the lights came on, George asked, poker-faced, "Do you want to go get a bite to eat?"

"You bastard. You know I want to go home and fuck."

George laughed, but he took me back to the dormitory, where he undressed me and fell on my wet pussy, quenching the raging flames with his cool tongue. We made love for hours until I was, at last, satiated.

I suppose it sounds as if George was cruel – but he knew that I thoroughly enjoyed his teasing. Many years and lovers later, I would often fantasize about being with a man who was absorbed in something else while fondling me absentmindedly. After George's phone call, I got to thinking about how to play out this fantasy.

Don and I have amassed an extensive collection of X-rated videos which we frequently watch to enhance our lovemaking. The next weekend, when the kids were at their grandparents' house, we sat in front of the VCR with the remote control at the ready. I asked Don to keep his eyes on the video and fondle me, but otherwise to pay me no attention. Always willing to play along with my fantasies, Don obliged. He put on an old Marilyn Chambers movie, knowing how much I respond to her enthusiastic vocal effects, and he sat back in an armchair, pulling me onto his lap. As Marilyn thrashed about, moaning and screaming, Don idly fondled my breast, his eyes glued to the set. I watched his impassive face as I got hotter and wetter, and I finally sank to my knees, exactly as I had done with George so many years ago in the planetarium. This time, however, I was not prevented from pulling out a thick cock, filling my mouth with the sweet meat, and sucking it down my throat.

I lapped and licked on Don's organ, my head bobbing up and down, Marilyn's sexy voice in my ear. Every once in a while I looked up at Don's immobile face. The rigidity of his dick was the only clue that he was in the least bit excited. He let me lick and suck while he watched the movie until, his cock twitching uncontrollably, he shot his come down my throat. I swallowed every drop, my eyes on his face, which usually crumbled in ecstasy when he climaxed; this time, though, he kept his features as still as if they'd been etched in stone.

58

I went wild. Panting and gasping, I desperately craved release. I climbed up and humped my cunt against Don's softening member. He tried to shove it into me, but alas, it would not stay. We've learned over the years that there's more than one way to fill a pussy though: Don laid me down on the floor, and, kneeling before me, entered me with his fingers. I bucked against them, looking at my husband's strong hairy chest, his biceps that rippled with every thrust. Meanwhile, the movie rolled on.

"Watch the video," I instructed.

Don turned his face toward the screen where Marilyn was stretched out on something resembling a massage table while a guy in black leather worked her over. I think he was dripping candle wax onto her nipples. I didn't give a shit what was happening on screen – Don could have been watching *The Sound of Music* for all I cared. What mattered was that he seemingly pay attention to something else while almost his entire hand – four fingers – worked my cunt, and his thumb pressed against my clit. I bucked and pushed against his hand, harder and harder, my head flung back, my tits thrust forward, and finally, just as Marilyn's voice reached an ecstatic crescendo, I found release.

As my orgasm subsided, Don laughed. "What was that all about?" he asked, leaning forward to kiss me.

I told him about George's phone call, and about the planetarium, hoping he wouldn't be too jealous. Don just laughed some more.

"Well," he said, "this opens up a whole new area, doesn't it?"

Indeed it did. Since that night, Don and I have played the teasing game in empty movie balconies, when he's driving the car, and – my very favourite – while he's coolly conducting business on the phone. But our biggest adventure is yet to come: on my next birthday, Don has promised to take me to the Hayden Planetarium.

Penny Candy

THE ONE-CENT PIECE is one of the most maligned of American coins. It weighs in the pocket, and can't – like it used to – buy you gum, parking, or sixty seconds through a Rocky Mountain viewer. It collects in little trays in convenience stores where the clerks can't be bothered to deal with the taxman. The penny still clogs up sink drains, and remains the most frequently swallowed coin of the American toddler. Not surprisingly, along with a clothespin and a poker chip, my sister found three of them in her broken VCR.

Once, minting pennies really was making something out of nothing. But now, inflation has transformed penny manufacturing into making next to nothing out of nothing. Strangely enough, however, people still flock to Denver to see Lincoln's head handily embossed on a round of copper, as if the minting of money was like watching water being turned into wine.

"Hey, Mickey!" A paper wad hit me in the shoulder. Instantly I turned and conveyed my disapproval to Jameson. "A coupla your kind on Channel One...."

Instinctively, I lowered the volume on my radio and turned my eyes toward the sidewalk monitor. It was one of the six screens I was responsible for. In its infinite wisdom, the U.S. Department of the Treasury had commissioned me to protect America's diminishing supply of pennies at the U.S. Mint in Denver. In general, tourists are a trustworthy lot, but around money, nefarious minds are always at work.

Levon J. loved to tease me about all the dykes on the security cameras, and over the years he'd gotten almost as good as me at spotting them. The women were just about to step out of frame, into the dead space between One and Two, but the admission line had slowed. On the control panel, I toggled the zoom lens for a closer look.

Pia Sheppard was suddenly in front of me in high relief. I recognized the layered brush of her greying blonde hair, since I've watched her a lot from the back, playing darts at Joker's on Thursday nights. Her biker jacket was open and she was laughing, and unself-consciously holding the hand of a woman I didn't recognize.

"Bingo," I muttered under my breath. I knew all of Pia's friends, I thought. "Must be an out-of-towner."

She was shorter than Pia, but not by much, and her dark hair was cut in a blunt pageboy. She was wearing dark glasses and a long trenchcoat. It was precisely the sort of disguise we'd been warned to watch out for at security school. I'd have suspected a sawed-off shotgun under the khaki had she not had both hands where I could see them. The two women were at the end of the tour line and I knew they wouldn't be joined by any other curiosity seekers for the day. They'd caught the last tour, the 2:45.

Over the stairway to the gallery in the stamping room, Channel Two picked them up again, lingering at the rail and pointing at the machines. Despite the absence of audio, I recognized from the sway of their shoulders that the rhythm of industry was having an effect on them.

They stood away from other tourists, and Maggie Holowaczyk, the docent, was preoccupied with the questions of some precocious eight-year-old triplets at the head of the small crowd. But they got my attention.

Even with their backs to the camera I could see that Pia had her arm inside the stranger's coat, perhaps jammed down the back of her coffee-colored cargo pants, fingering an elastic band of underwear, tracing along a hip, already wet herself. The girlfriend had her head turned slightly, and I caught the warning, impish gaze that asked, Just what do you think you're doing?

"Yo, Jameson," I said loudly.

I heard my buddy twist in his chair. "What?"

"Check this out."

Pia Sheppard is the most frustrating and exciting lover I've ever had, and I've had plenty. It's not that I'm loose, but fucking is an art, and I've got a creative side. I like the chase, the seduction, the tease, the bite.

It's not serious between us.

It started about three months ago, one night after my team was routed by hers at the dartboard; I bought her an Anchor Steam. That was the first clue that she had some class. At first I had my doubts about whether or not I was really attracted to her – she's not my usual type. She shoots darts in silk blouses and sexy heels; her skirt usually matches the jacket she's discarded. But it's just drag for work, she assures me. She's a tour guide on one of the buses that run out regularly to the foothills of the Rockies.

She didn't resist my invitation to come home with me that night, and I fucked her for hours, with my mouth and hands, on top and underneath and from behind. She came in copious, creamy shudders, biting her lip, or mine, or gasping a throaty, "Don't stop," until she passed out in the breaking dawn. I hadn't let her reciprocate. I'm a patient sort, and a little too butch to let down my guard early in the game.

In the succeeding weeks, however, she got more assertive and I let her, but I couldn't orgasm to save my life.

Channel Three caught them in the stairwell between stamping and sorting. They'd fallen a good ways behind their group, and Pia took advantage. She glanced furtively over her shoulder to make sure there was no one behind them. The lover's coat was open, and the front of her shirt unfolded over two of the most spectacular breasts I had ever seen. With a lascivious slowness designed to torture, Pia lowered her open mouth to a sallow nipple and hungrily stuffed the softness in. Pia pressed the woman's shoulders against the wall, and sucked at her like an angry stoat, denied enough. A hand raked through her hair, and her head moved to the other breast.

"Damn," breathed Jameson. He was standing behind my chair. He dug his hands deep into his pants pockets and fingered his change. "Is she going to do her right there?"

What the fuck was she doing? Maybe I shouldn't have been jealous – like I said, things between us aren't serious. But somehow, as I watched her saunter in the shadow off Camera Three, leaving her sweet young thing buttoning up and panting and saying something, I wondered what her agenda was. Then she was there again, grasping the woman's arm with an assured swagger, and once again, disappearing into the darkness.

There's dead space between Three and Four, a two-minute passage through the stacked pallets of coin bags and copper rods, down from the gallery and then onto the shop floor, where the sewing machines zip up five-dollar pouches. The tour group was already three minutes into the lecture by the time Pia and company emerged from the hallway. Pia had positioned herself so that the camera caught her dead on, but if she knew it was there she ignored it. Her back was turned three-quarters of the way away from her group, and she leaned in to whisper in her friend's ear.

Then she looked up, straight at the camera, expressionless, as she dropped a hand into her crotch, and she slowly massaged the inside of her thigh, as if she was packing. I watched her mouth the words: "I'm going to fuck you hard...."

Behind me, Jameson groaned. "Damn, this works for me." I heard him unbuckle his belt and quickly slip it out of his belt loops.

I rolled my eyes, but gestured toward the door. "Don't look at me to help you out, partner," I said. "Lock up if you are going to get off."

I had to admit, I was pretty fucking horny myself.

I looked back to the monitor. Pia had stepped in close to her new lover, as if a conversation of deep importance was about to take place. From my vantage point, I could see that she had unzipped her jeans, and that she was guiding her girlfriend's hand into her panties.

That's when I lost it, to be honest, because Pia has large hands. I find that moment – when my partner's finger just brushes the crease of my dripping vulva – to be excruciatingly erotic, and I could see that Pia was getting exactly such treatment. Pia likes to be in me, with one finger or four, teasing and tugging, pushing hard and slow, especially when I am standing. I like it too, until I can't stand anymore.

Jameson had had the decency to position himself a few feet away and behind me, and I heard his breath start to deepen and huff as he started to whack himself off. I have little interest in cocks, so I ignored him. I heard him mumble, Shit, she's in her pussy, and speed up his own action.

I moved to the edge of my own chair and unzipped my khakis and jammed my hand into my slippery slit. I wasn't going to waste any time, so I started my rhythmic thrum and felt my heart start to rev.

Pia's galpal looked nervous. The look on Pia's face was hard, determined, and she shifted her weight on her feet, and I felt the squeeze of her pelvic muscles on my own fingers. A hand found an upper arm, a grasp I knew. Then the girfriend withdrew, holding her sex hand awkwardly until Pia lifted it, and licked her own juice from her fingers.

The tour group had started to move again, the collective rumble of slow walkers turning in unison, and Pia zipped up. She was shaking a little, not with any kind of nervousness, but with the anticipatory kind of tremor that let's you know there's more to come.

At Channel Five I was hot, but Pia was nowhere to be seen. In shipping, the tourists crowded around the forklift track, as pallets of coin were stabbed and lifted, until the little trucks were nearly tipping over. Sweat ran down the nape of my neck and behind my ear. I was on the plateau, abuzz with hot engorgement, taking my strokes in practiced, long pleasure, not wanting to rush.

I scanned the screen, wishing I could see Pia, as if she might also be able to see me, and know what I look like on the veritable edge of coming.

The night before, with her tongue inside me, I had been begging, willing my cunt to swallow her, hoping that the pull and suck would never stop. But it did, and I hadn't finished. Pia had dressed in the semi-darkness, silently.

"Don't be angry," I'd said.

"I'm not," she'd answered too quickly. "I'm not sure why you're holding back."

"You can't really think that."

She shrugged. "Maybe it's me." A moment. A stare that could kill. "But I've never had this problem before."

What could I say? She slammed the front door as she went out.

I'd lost all sense of caring where she'd gone when Six picked them up in the lobby, lingering over the souvenirs and display cases of Penny Anomalies: Coins Gone Wrong. There, some penny sculptures and paper-thin coins made up a sort of Ripley's Believe It or Not of the weird and wonderful of Centiana.

I was solidly perched on my own three fingers, mixing and churning and waiting.

Pia looked pissed. She gestured at her girlfriend, sullen and threatening. The crowd had pretty much dispersed, and the lobby guard was trying not to listen in to whatever angry words were being exchanged.

I was seconds away from coming. If only Pia knew.

65

But suddenly, the girlfriend had hold of Pia's jacket, jerking it, and Pia reeled, turning toward the camera, and her hand went back, calculated her aim, and smacked the stranger's jaw in a hard, open slap. The girl staggered back a pace, and jostled a display, knocking a jar of pennies to the ground in a shattering rain of copper.

The camera caught Pia in a sly smile, and I came all over myself.

Frighten the Unicorns

LAWRENCE SCHIMEL

*I don't care where people make love, so long as they
don't do it in the street and frighten the horses.*
– Mrs. Patrick Campbell

DOESN'T IT MAKE YOU HORNY," Phil whispered in my ear as he
pressed up against me from behind, "to think of all those monks living here, visiting their neighbours' cells in the wee hours of the
night to teach each other the true meaning of devotion?"

My body responded instantly to his touch. It always takes me a
while to get used to someone, to the way their body works and fits
against mine, before I really respond to them sexually. In part, I
think it's because my body forgets what it's supposed to do during
the times I don't have sex, and has to relearn everything all over
again, every relationship. A body in motion stays in motion, and all
that. And in between relationships – when my body is at rest, as it
were – it learns to stay at rest. Sure, I jerk off all the time when I'm
not dating, but that's not the same thing; I can always respond to my
own fantasies, or to watching someone else having sex, on video or
in a magazine, and, especially, in real life.

Phil and I had been living together for almost two years now,
and my body was so highly attuned to him that I sometimes got a
hard-on from casual contact with him – if he so much as brushed
against me while I was doing the dishes, for instance. Feeling his
hard cock pressing up against my ass, even through two layers of
denim, my dick suddenly leapt to attention.

But this was no place to be having sex. "We're in public, dear," I
said, pulling away from him. "And anyway, this was a cloisters, as in
a nunnery, not an abbey for monks."

We were at the Cloisters Museum, having decided to escape the bustle of Manhattan without going through the hassle of actually leaving the island. There are dozens of little places like this throughout the city, pockets of calm and serenity that we almost never found the time for. But, on a spur of the moment decision, I'd taken the afternoon off from work and picked Phil up and dragged him up here on the subway, for a bit of culture and relaxation. Take the A train.

"Well, imagine it anyway," Phil continued. "Roomfuls of men, divorced from any contact with women for the pursuit of a higher thought, nothing to distract them from the buildup of semen in their balls, aching for release."

He'd moved up against me again, and his hand had crept around my waist, snaking its way into my front pocket, where he was squeezing the shaft of my cock as he spoke. It felt good, but I was afraid someone would notice us. "We're in a public courtyard," I repeated. I had nothing against public displays of affection, but I was concerned about pushing the bounds of propriety.

"They're not paying any attention to us," he said, adjusting his grip within my pocket to tickle my balls. He seemed to be correct; the courtyard was virtually empty, and the few people who were there seemed too preoccupied to notice us as they hurried inside to the dimly lit, air-conditioned room which held the tapestries. I stopped worrying for a moment and ground my hips backward to rub against his crotch. "And there are no horses for us to frighten," he continued. "Now, a unicorn is a different matter."

I laughed and Phil's voice deepened as he dropped back into the fantasy. "Think of all those poor little masochists, flagellating themselves for not being pure enough, as their minds kept dwelling on sin and their bodies followed after. Think of all of them, just desperate for a little discipline." He squeezed my nuts for emphasis, and I gasped for breath. My cock began to throb almost painfully with all the blood that was filling it now.

Phil was getting me all worked up on purpose, I knew, with the story and his groping. He loved having sex in unusual places, and the perversity of the situation must've really appealed to him, this blasphemous idea of practicing a bit of sodomy within the walls of a "sacred" and supposedly chaste place. And right then I wanted nothing more than to let him rip my clothes off and have sex right there, in full view of everyone. But the puritan in me made me drag

him off into one of the more remote courtyards and into the bushes. I'm very much a voyeur, and intellectually I think that there's an
economy of give and take, but in practice I'm just not much of an
exhibitionist.

As soon as I got Phil into a secluded corner, however, I was
down on my knees in front of him in an instant, unbuttoning his
501s. "That's it, my son," he said, playing the holy Father as his cock
sprang free from his jeans and lifted its head toward heaven. "Let
the spirit of the Lord fill you." I licked the shaft, working my way
from his fuzzy nuts up to the tip and back down again, loving that
strong taste and smell of sweat from his balls. I pulled it down so I
could lick the vein that snaked its way across the top, growing thick
just before it disappeared below the crown. I wrapped my fingers
around the base of his cock and flicked my tongue across the sensi-
tive rim of the crown, back and forth, teasing him until neither he
nor I could stand it any longer.

At last, I took his cock between my lips.

"Mmm, yeah," he grunted as he sank into the wet of my mouth.
"Can't you imagine it," Phil went on, "*The Unicorn Tapestries* from
Catalina Video, featuring Lex Baldwin repeating ad infinitum, 'Yeah,
suck that horn, suck that big horn.'"

I wanted to laugh, but couldn't with his cock so far down my
throat, so I just sucked harder as he chuckled and pumped his hips
so his cock slid in and out of my mouth.

Phil had always been very vocal during sex, and was always
cracking jokes about what we were doing. It had taken some getting
used to when we first started dating, since I wasn't used to men saying anything beyond the typical porn-movie grunts and lines. I'd
thought that was all there was to sex, actually, but now I really got
into Phil's verbal play. After all, sex is supposed to be fun.

"If we were really going to enact the tapestries, though," Phil
said, breaking off a branch from one of the nearby trees, "you'll need
this." I thought he meant to whip me with it, but instead he pulled
me off his cock until my lips were wrapped only about the crown –
I was unwilling to fully release him – and wrapped the prickly
branch about my neck like a collar. "Much better," he said, "your
crown of thorns. Who told you to stop sucking, boy?"

I didn't need any further prodding, and eagerly slid back down
his cock, ignoring the way the branch dug against my skin as his
cock swelled my throat. There are times when I'm sucking cock

69

when I'll go almost into a trance, and I've been surprised a few times by getting off from it without even touching myself. One thing I loved about Phil's cock was the way it was so perfect for my mouth. Which is not to say I could take all of him in – he was too long for that – but that's one of the reasons his cock was so perfect: it was a challenge, it left me always wanting more of it, trying to fit more of it down my throat. And I never got tired of trying.

Phil pulled his cock from my mouth, and turned to face the wall he'd been leaning against, dropping his pants as he changed position. I stayed on my knees, about to protest, until I realized what he was doing and eagerly buried my face in the crack of his ass once he'd exposed those muscled mounds to me. My tongue worked its way towards his asshole, licking until it found that tight bud, and I pulled his cheeks apart with my hands to reach more of it. His sphincter loosened under my tongue's constant probing and massaging, and I thrust my tongue into him, as deeply as I could. I pulled him toward me by his hips, until my nose was squashed flat against the flesh of his ass cheeks as I ate him out.

I could feel his asshole clench, involuntarily, around my tongue as he began to shoot thick ropes of jism against the cloister wall. I kept working my tongue into his ass as he pumped his cock dry, trying to keep my tongue inside him as his hips bucked each time he dropped a load. I couldn't get enough of him, and even after his body had stopped shuddering I licked at his asscheeks, nibbling at the smooth flesh and the downy hairs that coated them.

Without bothering to pull up his pants he fell to his knees beside me. "That was divine," he said, holding my face in his hands, before bringing my lips to his and kissing me. His tongue was warm and wet as it entered my mouth, and I wondered if he could taste himself on my tongue, the taste of his own ass. He flicked his tongue along the backs of my teeth as his hands slid down my body to pinch and twist my nipples, one and then the other, through the fabric of my shirt.

But he knew my cock was aching for him, so he didn't wait long before letting one hand drop to my crotch while the other continued to tease my nipples. He unzipped my jeans, not bothering to undo the belt. By this time my Calvins were damp with precome and longing, like they'd been dropped in the Hudson and put on without being wrung dry. He tugged them down and pulled my cock free at last, swollen with my desire for him. While Phil's cock stood at attention when he was erect, curving up toward his belly, mine was more direct, pointing straight out from my crotch. Not nearly as long as Phil's, it was thicker and had a solid heft to it. He held it lovingly in one palm and hacked a glob of spittle onto the head. With his thumb, he rubbed the saliva over the tip of my cock, pulling back the foreskin with his other hand to wipe away the precome that had pooled there. He spat again on my cock, rubbing his hand down the shaft to spread the saliva out, then without preamble took me into his mouth and began to suck.

I let out a moan and felt my knees would've buckled if we weren't already kneeling, as his lips closed around me and I was buried inside that warm, wet cavern of his mouth. My cock felt like it swelled even further to fill the vacuum created by his suction. His tongue began to rub the underside of the shaft, without letting his lips lose their lock around the base of my cock. For a moment, I tried to figure out if he were impaled upon my cock, or if I was the one who'd been captured by his lips, but I didn't really care, it felt so good. I could feel him swallow, the slick muscles at the back of his throat tightening and squirming around my thick tool, and he tried to take even more of me into himself, even though his nose was pressed flat against my belly and his lips were closed on that part of my shaft where the pubic hair crept onto the first half-inch. There was no place for him to go, so he just sucked even harder; I had to wonder how he could breathe like that. I would've hit my gag reflex long ago.

But it felt so good, and he didn't seem to have any problems breathing, so I stopped worrying about him and grabbed his hair. I broke the lock on his lips by pushing his head from me and pulling part-way out of his mouth, only to thrust my way back down his wet throat a moment later.

Without warning, Phil spat out my cock.

"And where do you think you're going?" I asked him, grabbing my dick in one hand and pumping myself with the lube from his saliva. It felt good to squeeze my cock more tightly than his lips could, but nothing like being surrounded by a fat wet tongue and mouth.

Phil didn't answer. He turned from me and pulled a condom and a small bottle of lube from his backpack.

"You were planning this all along, weren't you?" I asked.

Again, Phil didn't answer, just smiled and unrolled the condom over my cock. I should've realized Phil would see any excursion as a new, unusual location in which to have sex. I took the bottle of lube from him and poured a dollop onto my finger as he turned around and thrust his ass up to me again, holding on to a branch of the ornamental pear tree we were standing beneath in order to brace himself. I rubbed the lube over his puckered hole, already loosened by my tonguing, and then coated my finger with the viscous gel, rubbing it up and down along his crack where the lube clung, matting down the dark hairs. As I pressed my finger directly on the roseate bud of his asshole and began to massage it in a tight circle, I couldn't help thinking of it being like one of the stained glass rose windows so common in Christian architecture, including the cloisters around us.

Phil was in no mood for theological or architectural musings, however, and pushed backward against my finger. I slid into his ass up to my second knuckle where the finger widened, then began twisting my hand like a corkscrew as I pushed deeper into him. "You know why unicorns only like virgins?" I asked him.

Phil broke off moaning long enough to ask, "No, why?" as I twisted inside him. I pulled my fingers out so he could concentrate on my answer, and held the base of my cock against his hole as I prepared to reply.

"Because they like a tight piece of ass," I answered, and sunk into him. I fucked him in long, slow strokes at first, getting him used to my thick cock being inside of him before beginning to increase the pace.

"If you're the unicorn," Phil asked me as I was pumping into him, "how come I'm the one being ridden?"

"Just shut up and enjoy the ride," I answered. "Or I'll stop." I paused, half out of him, for emphasis, as if I could actually call things off right now without getting the worst case of blueballs I could imagine.

"Don't you dare," he said and reached back to grab my hips and pull me deeper into him. "Giddyap already."

I giddyapped, thrusting into him faster and faster. He was jerking himself off in time to my pumping. I was always jealous of the fact that he could get hard again so quickly after coming. I took forever to build to an orgasm, and once I had I was out of commission for a good while. Which led for some agonizingly pleasurable nights, since Phil loved trying to coax me into getting hard again right after I'd come.

72

I could feel myself on the verge, though, as if I were about to break into a gallop, I was tearing into Phil's ass so fast. My back broke a fresh sweat. I could smell the sweet scent of Phil's come still lingering in the air, from when he'd shot all over the wall, and thinking about eating him out again pushed me over into release. My cock spasmed inside him, squirting load after load of hot jism into the condom's reservoir tip. At last I came to a stop, my cock still buried deep inside him, and half-collapsed against him, trying to catch my breath. Phil began to beat himself off again while I was still within him, and a moment later he cried out and shot a second barrage of jism against the cloister wall.

"So this is why unicorns are so magical," Phil said as I pulled out of him. I slid the condom from my cock and tied a knot in it to keep the jism from spilling out. "A far cry from just a horse with a horn, I say." He handed me tissues from his backpack and wiped himself off before zipping up his pants.

"Next week we can go to the Claremont Stables on Amsterdam and 82nd," I said, pulling up my own jeans and looking about the still-empty courtyard, "see if we can't frighten the mundane horses."

Desire

RON SMITH

FOR A LARK, because we had nothing better to do, a friend, Karl
Singer, and I stood in the middle of the pavement at the corner of
Granville and Georgia, two main thoroughfares in Vancouver, and
looked up into the sky. At nothing. The old clock that had stood at
this intersection for years ticked on; people late for work or hurrying to business appointments detoured around us, some throwing us
hostile glances for causing them to swerve off an otherwise pur-
poseful course; and every now and again a driver honked his horn
in a blast of irritation – whether at us or at another driver, I wasn't
sure.

I noticed the mountains on the North Shore had finally lost their
cap of snow in the heat of the summer sun. And at the foot of
Granville, I could make out whitecaps on the inlet and the funnels
and flags of cruise ships. For a moment I speculated on the journeys
people take, how ships that put out to sea must become prisons of
hospitality, floating islands of desire.

We continued to scan the sky, a deep and luminous blue beyond
the thrust of the skyscrapers. Shadows filled the length of both
streets and a gentle breeze, like a ghost's breath, made the mid-
morning air feel cooler than it really was. At intervals, sunlight
would suddenly strike a face and the person's hand would shoot up
to shield his eyes. Or brilliant light would bounce off a shop window,
the glare blinding, leaving little sunspots dancing in your eyes. Karl
stretched his right arm upward, his jacket sleeve falling back and
forming a cowl around his shoulder. He pointed with his index finger towards the sky. Immediately I thought he looked as if he should
have been turned the other way round and painted on a chapel ceiling, his movement was so sudden and authoritative, so self-assured,

his limb seemingly detached from his body.

I peered up, my gaze following the direction of his arm, and nodded. I saw nothing, although instinctively I felt I must, even if only for an instant. By now my head was tilted so far back I feared I might lose my balance. Besides a certain degree of discomfort, I felt disoriented. Perhaps I did see a flash of light, something, anything, a daymoon faintly visible against a blue sky, the lonely orbit of an astronaut, a soul winging its way to heaven, that held my attention. After all, I was one of the architects of this scheme, not one of its dupes.

A man wearing a finely tailored, three-piece suit was the first to stop and join us. His curiosity was palpable. He set his leather briefcase down and immediately pointed his arm in the air. I looked at him in disbelief and then cast my eyes once again towards the sky. What was it he saw, I wondered?

Then an older, heavy-set woman, wearing a thick winter coat and a hat with a veil, almost knocked me over. She was so busy looking skyward, she miscalculated her steps and tripped on the curb.

What's up? she asked, stumbling and grabbing my sweater to steady herself.

I pointed, somewhat less enthusiastically than Karl or the man in the suit had, towards the sky.

Oh, she said, that's beautiful. Quite remarkable, don't you think? Her neck made accordion folds as she arched her back and brushed the black net away from her eyes and off her forehead.

I mumbled something unintelligible at her. Now there were three of them who saw whatever it was I was unable to see.

The cooling breeze died. Kitty-corner from us a small band of street musicians packed up their instruments and, like a family of gypsy street thugs, moved between the cars towards us, their fingers strumming the shadows.

The sun had shifted higher into the sky and the light reflecting off the buildings was dazzling.

Two young women came strolling along, arm in arm. They were dressed in bright, summer-coloured suits with short skirts. Their lips were full and moist and laughing. When they tipped their heads and squinted their eyes, gazing up into the sky, their long golden and auburn hair cascaded down their backs and brushed against the small of their arched backs. They jostled against Karl, who pretended not to notice them, but then nestled closer to them with his hips and legs and whispered something I was unable to hear. Their mouths made perfect "O"s. I gaped in amazement and thought to admonish him, but I was certain he knew how much I feared making a fool of myself with a woman.

The man wearing the suit rubbed the toe of his shoe on the back of his pant leg, shifting from one foot to the other, never once looking away from whatever held his gaze.

Soon, others joined us and we became a crowd of twenty or more people. We all stood on that spot, at that corner, looking up into the sky. At nothing, as far as I could see! The hands of the old clock rested on twelve.

Some pointed to objects they saw, confident of their vision. They reported cloud formations in the shapes of sheep or ships or unicorns or gods of whatever design filled their minds. They saw birds – swallows, pigeons, crows, sparrows – circle and dive between the buildings that fashioned the canyon floor where we stood. They saw aircraft. And a few saw an inexplicable light.

For a time I was skeptical about what they said they saw, especially when I watched a woman lean out a window eight floors up and empty a pitcher of water into the sky above our heads, but with time I was convinced that what they said they saw, I, too, could see, with a little effort.

As hard as I concentrated, all I got for my exertion was a headache.

At that moment, just when I thought my neck would permanently kink from straining to look at the heavens, a young redhead tapped me on the shoulder. Her face was sprinkled with freckles.

I've been watching you, she said.

A trolley bus passed by noiselessly. A cyclist wheeled around the corner, his legs pumping effortlessly.

What is it you desire, she asked, really desire?

Oh, I said, because I did not know her, a little of this, a little of that.

I see, she said. I've been watching you from the start, from when you first took up your position on the corner. I know what you and your friend are up to.

I pretended not to understand what she was saying. As sore as my neck was, I leaned back and looked up once again into the sky.

Don't treat me like the others, she said.

She was tall. Her long fingers caressed the surface of a locket she wore around her neck. With me, she said, there is a difference between what you think you can do and what can be done. If you want to kiss me, go ahead! Don't just think about it! Otherwise all you have is the thought.

Words rolled around in her mouth like hard toffee.

She pressed the clasp on the locket and opened it.

What do you see, she asked?

Nothing, I said.

No, no, she said. Her eyes were blue and endless, and her voice wrapped around me, lingering. You must look more carefully. More closely.

I did.

And what I thought I saw was a tiny mosaic insert that in the flickering sunlight of the street looked like a portrait of me.

Sightseer

EVERYTHING WAS DARK. Dark and still.

He was walking – being led, rather – down echoing corridors, corridors he couldn't see. It's where his sense of adventure had gotten him. His sense of adventure and his hard dick.

It had started, as so many Roman stories must have started, on the Spanish Steps. It had started, as so many Roman stories must have started, with a glance from dark brown eyes.

"How are you?" the man's deep Italian voice had asked. Jason knew what it meant. Jason was young, but he was neither stupid nor innocent. Nor was he enamored of his dorm room at the shabby hostel, ten college-age backpackers bedded down side-by-side in a stuffy room of what must have been a nobleman's villa a long time ago. A long, long time ago.

Jason, who was stoned, had been staring absently at a fountain shaped like a sinking ship. Now he looked up into dark brown eyes. The man was old, mid-thirties maybe. And not particularly good-looking. Not really homely, just ordinary. But well-dressed. And therefore rich. Not that Jason was out for money, not exactly. But he'd parlayed his good looks and wrestler's body into some nice meals and a bit of spending cash while he was at Dartmouth, careful not to let his frat brothers know. And there'd been that guy around his age in Paris; he'd stayed with him almost a week in his flat on the Place des Vosges. He never went out of his way for any of this; it just came to him....

"Fine," said Jason, and smiled, and got ready to rise to his feet.

"Would you like some dinner?" It was only late afternoon, but the guy didn't believe, apparently, in fucking around.

Jason smiled. Paydirt.

The sports car was a Lamborghini, not that Jason would have recognized it; he found out from the name plate. And the restaurant was a good one, near the racetrack-shaped Piazza Navona.

So far so good, thought Jason, as he bit into butter-soft veal. An expensive dinner in a place where the headwaiter knew the name of Jason's "friend" – *Signore* DeAngelis, Paolo – and where the excellent wine and tender baby calf were being paid for out of someone else's pocket. Jason found himself wondering if this Italian guy had done this sort of thing often, if he was just one of an endless parade of horny young backpackers from Perth and Prague and New York, boys that Paolo had tried to pick up and fuck.

The conversation was polite, friendly, slightly awkward on Jason's part, though DeAngelis never stumbled. Since the subject of lire never came up, Jason figured money wasn't going to change hands, which was fine with him. He was glad to spend the evening in some place besides that lousy hostel full of clueless, clumsy straight boys. The gate to the hostel was locked at ten o'clock, but he should have no problem talking this guy – Paolo – into letting him stay the night, unless he....

"Huh?" Jason said. He'd missed whatever Paolo had asked.

"I said, are you ready to leave?"

Paolo paid the bill without flinching. They left the still-half-empty restaurant, the valet brought the Lamborghini 'round, and they set off into the Roman evening. Jason didn't ask where.

They were driving toward the Ponte Sant'Angelo, the bulk of the ancient *castello* hulking on the opposite shore of the Tiber, when Paolo asked, "Do you like surprises?" Baroque angel statues gestured toward the Lamborghini, heavenly simpers frozen on their faces.

"Sure, I like surprises," said Jason. He did.

"Then put this on." Paolo handed him a blindfold, the kind they give you on first-class airplane flights. It was a weird request, but Jason had heard weirder, and some of them he had obeyed.

"Do you understand Italian?" asked Paolo.

"The only words I know are 'pizza' and 'ciao'."

"Fine," Paolo said. Jason heard the beeps of a cell phone, then Paolo's half of a conversation. His voice was firm and quiet; the only word Jason caught for sure was *ciao*.

"You trust me?" DeAngelis asked Jason.

"Yes," Jason said. No, he thought, or not sure. But he figured he could take care of himself pretty well, and besides, he liked an adventure. A bit of excitement, danger even. And besides that, Paolo's hand was between Jason's legs, kneading his inner thigh, just inches from the American's dick, which was hard.

The car made its way through the soft Italian night for a little while, then pulled to a sudden stop.

"We're here," said Paolo DeAngelis. "If I guide you, can you walk with the blindfold on?"

"No problem," Jason said.

The Italian got out of the car, walked around to Jason's door, and guided the young man to his feet.

"Wait here," Paolo commanded. Jason did, dick still half-hard. Paolo walked off, had a brief, hushed conversation with someone, then came back and grabbed him by the elbow. "This way."

Jason heard a heavy door swing open on its hinges, then slam shut behind them after they'd passed a few paces on.

Very little light leaked in beneath the blindfold; wherever they were, it was dimly lit. After being led through corridors, down ramps and up a flight of stairs, he was beginning to wonder just what the hell this surprise was. He was beginning to worry. He was starting to think he should have just suggested screwing in a suite at the Hotel Excelsior.

"We're here," Paolo said. "Stand still." The Italian's hand left his elbow. From beneath his blindfold, he saw that lights had been turned on. And now Paolo was back. "Strip," he commanded Jason.

Jason did as he was told, awkwardly, since he was standing unsupported, and he couldn't see. Naked, he shivered. There was cold stone beneath his feet. Paolo pushed him backwards, up against a chilly metal grille.

"Put your hands above your head."

Jason, half playing along, half in earnest, asked, "And if I don't?"

In answer, he felt a cold metal blade against his throat.

"I'll kill you," Paolo said.

Jason raised his hands. Paolo wrapped rope around the American's wrists, binding them together, tying them to an upright bar of the grille. Jason might have fought back, torn the blindfold off, tried to overpower Paolo, grab the knife, run. He didn't. Instead, he just hung there, naked. Like Saint Sebastian. Like Saint Sebastian with a hard-on.

He heard Paolo spit, felt one warm, wet hand wrap itself around his cock while the blade, in the other hand, returned to his throat.

The guy was crazy, Jason knew, fucking crazy, but it was an adventure. And adventure was better than nothing.

Paolo's hand had a direct line to Jason's pleasure centres. Even in his fear and uncertainty, Jason felt close to coming. It was as though his dick was disconnected from his mind; it was a feeling he'd had several, no, many times before.

Paolo said something. Something in Latin. "Sorry," Jason said. "I'm lapsed. My Latin's a bit rusty."

The edge of the knife bit into his throat. The Italian leaned close and whispered in his ear.

Jason must have misheard. "What?" he asked.

DeAngelis repeated: "You are the Light of the World."

The knife pulled away from his throat, dropped with an echoing clatter on the stone floor. A large room, then. Where was he?

"Where am I?" he asked.

Paolo's hand left his dick. Put it back! part of him wanted to beg.

The blindfold came off.

Jesus, risen in triumph, raised his arm above his head in a muscular gesture that condemned the damned to hell. Saints and martyrs swirled about him. The dead rose from their graves. The damned, dark in sin, were ferried down the River Styx.

Jason blinked. It was Michelangelo's titanic painting of the Last Judgment.

They were in the Sistine Chapel. Jason was tied, naked, to the choir screen of the Sistine Chapel.

"What ... how?"

"It helps to have money. Rome may not be totally corrupt, but everything can be bought. Everything. And an archbishop who wants his secrets kept is never ungrateful."

"But, Jesus ... here?" For a sudden, giddy moment, Jason thought of Charlton Heston in a false beard, supine on a scaffold, painting the Sistine ceiling while white gobs of something – paint? – dripped onto his face.

DeAngelis, still fully dressed, sank to his knees, looked up prayerfully at Jason's gleaming face, and took the young man's dick into his mouth. As good as Paolo's handjobs were, his blowjobs were even better.

Take, eat, this is my body, thought Jason, and felt like giggling again. And he felt like coming. "Wait, wait, wait. Back off," he said. Across the room, some near-naked martyr glared at him.

Paolo's mouth slipped from his dick and moved to his balls. The kneeling Roman nuzzled between Jason's thighs, his tongue moving back toward the young man's hole. Jason spread his feet farther apart, thrust his thighs forward. Paolo shifted around so his tongue could lick Jason's hole. The tip thrust inside him. It felt great, just great.

"Fuck me," said Jason. Across the chapel, Jesus sent the unrepentant to perdition. The fires of Hell.

Paolo rose to his feet. He had the knife in one hand again and his dick, sticking through the fly of his expensive trousers, in the other. Sliding the blue steel blade between Jason's tender wrists, he sliced through the rope. Jason's arms were free.

DeAngelis removed his sport coat and laid it on the cold stone floor. Paolo gestured downward with the knife. Jason lay on his back, mostly on the sportcoat, his legs spread, his knees in the air.

Slowly, carefully, Paolo undressed, folding his clothes, piling them neatly next to his supple Italian loafers. When he was naked, big uncut cock sticking stiffly before him, he stared down at the boy lying there, a weird look of joy on his dark Italian face. He said something else in Latin. This time, Jason didn't ask for a translation. Paolo dropped to his knees, kneeling between Jason's thighs. Paolo was hairy, which Jason liked, and had a thick, well-muscled body. The kind of body that could do harm.

At last, Jason allowed himself to look at the ceiling. He'd been meaning to see the Sistine Chapel, ever since arriving in Rome a week ago. But he'd always found something else to do. Like hanging out on the Spanish Steps. Like going to dinner with a filthy-rich man in a Lamborghini.

And now he lay there naked, the fresco looming above him. Prophets. Angels. Women who looked like men; Michelangelo was a fag, Jason seemed to remember. The coldness of the hard floor seeped through the sportcoat. Jason shivered again.

Paolo's hands grabbed Jason's ankles, forcing his legs back and up, up into the air, toward the ceiling, toward heaven.

Remembered scenes, stories from Jason's childhood. The flood, Noah's flood, animals two-by-two. Noah, later, drunk; after saving the world, a guy's entitled to party. David and Goliath, over in the corner, the boy's sword upraised, off with the giant's head. And everywhere prophets, grim and forbidding.

Lying there, looking up, Jason felt Paolo's dick against his hole, and idly wondered if the man had a condom on. He stared again at David, the blade's expected thrust.

Paolo spit into his palm, smeared it into Jason.

The serpent, strong and swelling, curled around Eden's tree, Evil with a human face, offering up the fatal fruit.

Paolo's dick pressed into him. Not enough lube, a moment of stabbing pain, then Jason relaxing, taking in the man's flesh. Paolo pulled out, stroked in again, pumping, pumping at him.

The Angel of God, telling Adam to get lost.

The stroking inside him. It hurts, he wanted to say. He didn't.

Adam hid his face from the Angel of the Lord.

It hurt.

Paolo slapped Jason's cheek.

Jason thought of Father D'Onofrio. Back when he was just ten years old, Father D'Onofrio....

It hurt.

The priest's hands....

"Cursed is the ground for your sake ..."

Paolo slapped Jason again.

"... and darkness was on the face of the deep."

God stretched his hand out.

Jason thought of the man in Verona, a middle-aged business-man.

"Fuck me," said Jason.

As the man slept, Jason stole the businessman's wallet and started to creep out of the room.

Adam stretched his hand out.

Paolo grunted into his thrusts. Jason, gaze shifting from the ceil-ing to the man's face, saw ... what?

The man woke up. Jason punched him.

God stretched his hand out.

The man cried.

Jason flailed his arms, hands, felt Paolo's knife lying on the floor. Cold steel.

Paolo shot into Jason's ass.

Hot as flame.

"Take me," said Jason.

Their fingers touched.

Their fingers touched.

And in the morning, the museum guard found the American

boy on the floor of the Sistine Chapel, tears dried on his cheeks, curled up in a fetal position, lying naked on an Armani jacket, the Hand of God stretched out above his head.

St. Stephanie

THOMAS S. ROCHE

I WAS OUT OF BREATH after the first hundred steps. My lungs burned, my head swam, I thought I glimpsed Jesus in an alcove.

I was sure that an ascent like this wouldn't normally leave me this breathless – but we had been running around all morning, visiting museums and churches, trading expletives each time we experienced the stunning beauty of the ostentatious Austrian architecture. And now we were ascending to heaven on the wings of angels – yeah, right. More like the rubbery legs of an overextended California college student. I swore to myself I would try to get more exercise if I survived this.

"Hurry up," she called playfully from behind and beneath me. "This place is named after my patron saint. You want him to think I'm engaged to a slowpoke?" She swatted me on my ample *derrière*.

St. Stephansdom, Vienna, Austria. More steps than you can count up to the top of the steeple, each one seemingly higher than the last. Three o'clock in the afternoon, the middle of August, an afternoon unseasonably hot for Vienna – even this time of year. I wished I'd taken Stephanie's advice and worn shorts.

"Hurry up!" chirped Stephanie, slapping me on the ass. "God can't wait all day, you know." Stephanie was a competition cyclist, having ridden from San Diego to Seattle before she was sixteen. She topped that by being captain of the high school rowing team for her junior and senior years and winning several cycling races. Currently she was making plans to hike the Appalachian Trail, something like 3,000-plus miles of wilderness from Kentucky to Maine, but "I don't think I'll do it all in one summer," she had told me. I'm sure she was joking. Wasn't she?

Now, at nineteen, Stephanie rode her bike everywhere. She also ran every morning, went swimming every night.

I occasionally did a push-up.

I stopped, looked down, eyed her disapprovingly. She smiled back at me, batting her lashes innocently.

"I've got to rest," I growled without conviction.

"Fuck that," she laughed. "What does not kill you makes you stronger. Didn't Schwarzenegger say that?"

Stephanie was a science major, obviously. I was a triple major in philosophy, history, and literature.

"It wasn't Schwarzenegger," I told her with a smirk. "It was Dolph Lundgren."

"Oh. Was he Austrian?"

"I don't think so."

"Oh. Well, who cares, it still applies," she piped. "Come on, it's up or down, Jimbo. Trust me," she said with a mischievous smirk. "The view from the top is worth it. You'll thank me. Now move your ass, or I'll slap it again – oh, but you'd like that, wouldn't you, Jimbo? Come on, move it."

"I'm going down."

"No you're not. Don't chicken out. My man is strong like bull. Tell you what," she encouraged cheerfully, "I'll go first. That way you can take your time." She deftly darted past me and ran past a nun and a guy with a Johnny Cash t-shirt. Then she was gone, tapping her way up the incredibly-steep staircase.

I looked forlornly after Stephanie and began to run, wasting only a little breath with my grumbling.

I made good time after her, closing fast. Stephanie was leaping up the stairs like this was a game; it wasn't easy to keep up. I managed to stay less than ten feet behind her, and I even started to get closer. Nine feet. Eight. Seven. Then five. My heart was pounding, and my breath felt like fire in my lungs. I looked up at Stephanie's glorious, toned legs, pumping like the pistons of some finely-tuned machine.

Which is when I realized I could see right up her skirt.

Stephanie was wearing this short little plaid number, daring in its brevity – entirely decent on level ground, but an exhibitionist's fondest dream on the steep spiral staircase of St. Stephansdom.

She wasn't wearing much underneath – just a little black g-string. What had inspired her to wear such a slight undergarment today? Was it the weather? Certainly the unusual heat and humidity were the reason Stephanie had worn the tiny skirt – the only skirt she had brought to Europe in her well-ordered backpack. ("In case we go out," she had told me on the flight over. "Somewhere nice.") She had passionately encouraged me to wear shorts – but I had "known better," telling her "a breeze might come up." "I hope it does," Stephanie had answered enigmatically, her fingertips flirting with the hem of her skirt.

With a new burst of energy, Stephanie picked up speed.

"This is great," she said, barely even breathing hard. "There's no one in front of us now, so I can go as fast as I want. You still back there, Jimbo?" She always called me "Jimbo" when she was trying to annoy me.

Stephanie's whirling legs carried her up, out of my line of vision. Ignoring the agonies of my body in consideration of its more esoteric needs, I stepped faster.

Closer ... closer....

Finally it came back into view: The tiny string of fabric between the glorious majesty of those slender, smooth thighs, working back and forth against each other in an unavoidably suggestive rhythm. When she moved just so, I could glimpse the flexing tightness of her ass. Her g-string didn't hide much, and as her thighs pumped, it seemed as if the undergarment snuggled more firmly between the lips of her sex, almost as if those lips were becoming gradually more swollen....

"Faster!" she giggled, picking up speed. "Show 'em what we Yanks are made of!"

If I had not been so otherwise occupied, I would have groaned. But I fought back the pain and the exhaustion that were threatening to consume me. Stephanie danced forward and up, out of sight again – and I stifled the screams in my legs as I battled to keep up with her. I caught sight of her again, her skirt riding up higher on her thighs and making my job just a bit easier. Lord, how delicious those thighs looked, sheened with sweat, those wonderful, tight buns, bare under the tiny skirt, everything swirling together with her wonderful pussy there, beckoning me to heaven, coaxing me to greater heights of self-torture. My head felt like it would explode, but every time I was about to succumb to the exhaustion, I would catch a new angle, a fresh glimpse of Stephanie's crotch, and I would work my legs faster, like a marionette on a string.

As we climbed, it seemed like more of her crotch became visible ... as if the already tiny triangle of her g-string grew narrower, tighter, smaller.

Almost as if she were swelling.

I was sure of it. I could actually see her vaginal lips, which I couldn't when this mad chase started. And it wasn't my imagination. They were plainly there – evident in all their full, rouged glory, pink and swollen, curving around the tightness of the g-string as if holding it in the most unbreakable of caresses.

"Feeling better?" She laughed down at me. "Getting your second wind?"

"You could say that," I told her, in a voice hoarse with desperation, croaking its way out of a throat thick with mucus.

"Good, good, goooooooood," she sighed, climbing still faster.

What had led her to wear such a small skirt and a revealing undergarment when she knew she would be walking around exerting herself all day? Certainly it couldn't be comfortable, that tight g-string riding up her crotch and her ass all day, working its way between her lips, rubbing and abrading her clit mercilessly....

I was starting to get hard.

Stephanie was not particularly inclined to wear underwear to begin with – she often went without, especially during the three seasons a year when she wore shorts nonstop. And her years of constant exercise – cycling, swimming, running, surfing – had left her with a body even more lean, taut, and slender than the one genetics had given her. Her tiny breasts hardly needed a bra. "I own one of those fucking things," she once told me with a sneer. "I wear it to weddings and funerals."

But who was she kidding? We both knew that it wasn't just comfort that made Steph go without. She was a shameless exhibitionist. Even if her breasts didn't require a bra for support, her nipples could have used a garment all their own. This did wonders for my libido – the frequent sight of Stephanie's nipples hardening under a t-shirt or a spandex racing jersey was enough to set my heart to pounding. And the all-but-constant knowledge that she didn't have a stitch on under her shorts, sweats, or jeans was a welcome one for me. The fact that I was also a shameless voyeur only increased Stephanie's shamelessness in her exhibitionism. There was something extremely hot about catching a glimpse up Stephanie's skirt when we were in public, or seeing her in a see-through tank-top at the beach. Something made it so exciting to me, even though I could have taken her back to the hotel and looked at her pussy for hours.

But it was being in public, and catching that "forbidden" glimpse, that excited me so.

"Mach Schnell! Schnell!" she giggled, running faster as I sought desperately to keep up with her. Now I was fully hard, my face bright red from the combination of exertion and arousal. The tourists passing me didn't seem to notice the bulge in my too-tight jeans (I would have to lay off the strudel) – but the material was pulled firmly enough across my crotch that the constant up-and-down motion of my legs was rubbing my head rapidly against the denim – rubbing it, rubbing it, rubbing it.

"Faster! Faster!" But Stephanie herself was slowing, and I could hear from the tone of her voice that she was tired – or was it exhaustion, after all? I began to slow myself.

And then Stephanie took off again as if out of a starting gate, running faster and faster up the stairs and giving me a perfect view of her crotch again – her lips swollen, red, working back and forth as she stumbled and fell to one knee just as I felt my cock exploding in my pants, spasms of pleasure flooding me as the front of my jeans acquired a dark stain.

"Oh my God," gasped Stephanie, now down on both knees. "Jesus."

We had made such good time that there was no one behind us for many yards. But there were still intermittent downward-bound tourists, and I didn't think the religiously-inclined among them would appreciate Stephanie's profanities – especially not the guy with the JESUS SAVES baseball cap and the PEACE THROUGH SUPERIOR FIREPOWER t-shirt. So I quickly untucked my t-shirt, glad that it was a long one, smoothed it over my crotch, and bent over to help Stephanie back to her feet. There was only another ten yards, perhaps, to the tiny room at the top of the steeple – and Steph and I made it together, leaning heavily upon each other. We had to be nudged through the final doorway by a giggling horde of Japanese girls garbed head to toe in fashionable Hello Kitty accessories.

––––––––

In the small room at the top of the steeple, Stephanie and I stood in front of one of the small, glassless windows and leaned against what passed for a sill.

Leaning forward, looking out the window at the magnificent view, I cradled Stephanie from behind, my arms around her waist.

"Did you really …?" I began to ask her.

"Find out," she whispered. I manoeuvered my body to hide what I was doing from the tourists coming into the room behind me. Deftly, I slipped a hand up the inside of one of Stephanie's thighs, guiding a finger between her lips … feeling how wet and slick she was. More importantly, feeling the tightness she always had after an orgasm.

I let my finger trail out of her and licked it surreptitiously.

"You did," I sighed.

"Uh-huh," she whispered, perplexed. "It's not like I planned it .. . well, I planned most of it," she giggled.

"Wicked. You are wicked. Any more sacrilegious plans for the afternoon?"

"No plans at all," she said. "Except going back to the hotel and yanking this string out of my ass. It's been crawling up there all day."

"I was wondering about that," I said.

"Ready to go down?" she asked.

"Not until we get back to the hotel room," I told her, which elicited a giggle.

"I think you should go first."

I smiled. "This is the old world, my dear. Ladies first."

Stephanie's mouth dropped open. "And you're saying I'm wicked?" she giggled.

"We'll talk," I said, and started down the stairs ahead of her. As I descended in tiny, tight circles, I said a silent prayer to St. Stephan – the patron saint of stonemasons, builders, and horses. Stephanie took her time behind me.

Steam

INA PROEBER

GERMAN? ENGLISH? FRENCH?"

"What's your name?"

"Married?"

The slim woman pushed her way through the gradually tightening circle of dark-haired men who offered themselves as guides in front of the Blue Mosque.

"Cassandra. I have three children," she said to quell their thirst for questions. She knew she'd better be polite and patient with these black-eyed men with their fiery gazes. They were attracted to her fair complexion like seagulls to the fresh fish caught off the shores of the Bosphorus.

A chilly breeze descended from the minarets of the mosque and played with the strands of blonde hair that had slipped out from under her scarf. She pushed forward, harder.

"Best guide!" they shouted after her in broken English.

"Very cheap!"

"I show you!"

Hoping to lose her last pursuer, Cassandra slipped into the entrance building of the Basilica Cistern and descended the stairs into the enormous cavern. The sound of water dripping into the pool echoed off the maze of identical columns and paced the time. She was alone in the cool stillness. Ink-black water cast back the indirect light in various shades of grey, and she felt as if she was wandering through the underworld.

Surrounded by dancing black shadows, Cassandra found herself standing in front of the illuminated head of the Medusa. She stared at the reflection of the sculpted face in the mirroring water. The face was feminine, with full, sensuous lips, and rounded contours. In

Medusa's eyes, though, Cassandra saw the famous petrifying glare.

The sound of footsteps on wet wood startled Cassandra. She turned. One of the guides had followed her into the deserted underground palace.

Cassandra's blood pounded. Her ears buzzed. Her body began to stiffen in the chill of fear. At the very last moment before his gaze could numb her completely, she dashed passed him, ran over the swaying pontoon, and fled the cistern.

Outside, the frigid air brought her to her senses. Without taking the time to look at her map, she disappeared into the tangle of side streets and lanes. Hunched over, her scarf tightened around her head, she zigzagged through passages too narrow for cars. Houses leaned toward her, almost touching her with their low eaves. Gaping entrance doors oozed a mouldy smell that mixed with whiffs of cooked, spicy food, reaching for her to draw her inside. When she saw the sign *Hamami* – Turkish bath – she knew there she would be safe from male pursuers and could calm her confused soul.

In this world of warmth and tranquility, three women lingered around the reception desk. Their bodies were massive and plump, wrapped in shapeless cotton tunics. One woman greeted Cassandra in Turkish and with an inviting gesture. In the glow of an Oriental lamp that hung from the domed ceiling, Cassandra saw a welcoming smile glide over the woman's lips.

Cassandra knew little about the customs and manners of Turkish baths. She could not ask the women for advice for they didn't share the same language. When she was shown to a cubicle to undress, she quickly read in her guidebook about the pleasures she would be treated to over the next hours.

Sitting in a niche with a marble basin, Cassandra scooped hot water over her body while her eyes wandered through the *hararet*, the steam room. Natural light filtered through the star-shaped skylights that covered the dome. Grandiose columns rose from the marble floor to the curved ceiling, giving the room a peaceful symmetry. Enshrouded in clouds of steam and obscured by columns, two other women soaked in the comfort of heat and solitude.

The woman Cassandra had met in the reception area served her a tiny cup of steaming coffee on a tray, then slipped away noiselessly. The black elixir was strong and sweet and awakened Cassandra's senses. She felt the hot marble against her naked skin and the heat inside her increase with every scoop of hot water.

Sweat trickled between her breasts and pooled on her belly. She lost herself in the indulgence of the experience.

Through the haze of saturated air, Cassandra saw the same woman signal her to come over to a basin on the far side of the octagonal room. The woman had shed her tunic. Ripe, bell-shaped breasts hung over the folds of her belly. Her skin, the colour of sandalwood, was flawless and firm. The diminutive panties she wore almost disappeared under her luxurious stomach.

With a sudsy mitten, the woman began to work on Cassandra's body: lathering, scrubbing, and stroking. The coarse fabric was merciless on Cassandra's tender skin, but the gentle touch of the woman's bare hands suggested admiration for the delicate flesh of her body. She pressed Cassandra's arms and legs against her opulent bosom and belly and indulged in her own hedonistic pleasures. Their two bodies merged in the confluence of soap and water.

Cassandra looked into the woman's face and was reminded of the image of the Medusa: feminine, rounded contours, sensuous lips, and glaring eyes – the same face she had seen in the cistern. This time, it was animated and painted in vivid shades of brown. And it was not fear that petrified Cassandra. It was the awakening of feelings, the stirring of hunger, and the answer to a lifelong riddle.

On the marble slab in the centre of the *hararet*, Cassandra lay spread-eagled on the heated surface. The woman never spoke a word to her. With gentle gestures she turned Cassandra's body as she constantly hummed a melody as if in prayer. The sultry air, the hands kneading her body, the heat radiating from the woman's breast resting on Cassandra's buttocks lulled her in a state of letting go.

Too soon the massage was over. Cassandra retreated to the cubicle and stretched out on the ottoman. The small room lay in semi-darkness. A shaft of dim light came through the ornate carving in the upper part of the door and fell on the dark-brown wood paneling. From the upholstery and the Oriental blanket that covered her naked body rose the smell of soap, dust, and fragrant hair. She rendered herself to the sleepiness that had taken hold of her.

Cassandra woke to the snap of the lock on the door. The masseuse entered the cubicle, locked the door, and drew the faded curtain. She was dressed in a bathrobe, fastened by a belt around her waist. Her impressive thighs pushed the fabric apart and exposed the black, curly hair of her groin.

Murmuring in a low voice, she knelt down on the floor beside the ottoman. She gently touched Cassandra's pale lips, followed the line of the eyebrows, and ran her fingertips down the chiselled neck.

Cassandra was still waking from her numbing sleep and felt the sweet sensations through the veil of a dream. Heat rose into her face. The woman's voice was a throaty whisper, the timbre of cooing pigeons. Her sound was becalming, her touch arousing. Cassandra knew she was in a safe harbour.

The woman slowly removed the blanket. With her cool, moist lips she breathed kisses on Cassandra's breast. Shivers tingled over Cassandra's skull and hardened her nipples. The fingertips of the woman's left hand hovered over the dip of Cassandra's stomach; her touch light and sensual. When she reached the loins, a flutter spilled through Cassandra's body, forcing her to take a deep breath. Her heart beat faster.

The woman sucked Cassandra's erect nipples, cooled the moist skin with her breath, and let her tongue play around their aureola, causing Cassandra to shudder. She then slipped her finger between Cassandra's legs and pried them apart. Cassandra was no longer able to control her desire. She spread her legs and surrendered herself to the pleasures.

The heat of the succulent body beside her, the fire of the woman's touch, ignited Cassandra's lust. She wanted to feel the woman's flesh with her fingers, caress her skin, seize those luxurious breasts. She slipped one hand in the opening of the bathrobe. The woman quickly untied the belt, and her drooping breasts spilled over Cassandra's stomach. She caught their weight and fullness with her palm. The nipples, as large as pebbles and as red as cherries, protruded from the woman's breasts like the clapper in a bell. Cassandra rolled them between her fingers and dug her nails into the spongy texture. The woman no longer babbled her psalms, but moaned in long sighs.

Her fingers dipped into the moist cavity between Cassandra's legs. First one, then two, then three fingers slithered into the chasm, extracting the sweet juices. The woman began slowly to circle her fingers in the warm, fleshy folds. When she moved her head to the blonde fleece, Cassandra arched her back and lost hold of the swelling breasts. With her tongue and teeth, the woman evoked blessed contractions in Cassandra's loins. The subtlety of the touch was incomparable to anything she had experienced before.

The woman's fingers rotated faster and brisker, her mouth sucked harder and hungrier, and her tongue gave playful pauses. When Cassandra wanted to cry out in pleasure, the woman covered Cassandra's mouth with her voluptuous breast. Cassandra burst and buckled, and then let go.

The soothing hands retreated and covered her in the blanket again. Her eyes closed, Cassandra heard the snap of the lock. She felt warmth in every cell; a golden halo surrounded her body. Utter contentment lulled her back into sleep.

Dr. Holl's Adventures in Wonderland

FRIDAY AFTERNOON IN THE SEX CAPITAL OF THE WORLD found Dr. Gloria Holl hard at work in San Francisco's Advanced Study of Human Sexuality laboratory, located on top of one of San Francisco's lovely foothills.

Bone tired she was. But the competition was stiff, and Dr. Holl accomplished much when the bustling lab quieted down. While her students were calling it a day, the world's foremost sexologist sought to uncover the remaining mysteries of the human female sexual response.

Not wanting to be distracted by the rowdy crowd in the hall, she closed the laboratory door. She was close to a breakthrough discovery on the female orgasm. Just one more run-through of the video, *The Phenomenology of Orgasmic Involution and Associated Lubricities*. Would that all the orgasms she had viewed been hers. None were. No. Dr. Holl, top sex doyenne, was, of all things, pre-orgasmic. If her followers knew, it would demolish her reputation. It was her dirty little secret.

She glanced at her watch. Half past four. She took a break to peer at nearby Nob Hill. In the dead of winter, myriad lights already flickered, draped on the city's multiple breasts like tinsel. She felt lonely for a moment.

She twisted the mini blinds shut and ran the video.

Here we see the clitoris at the unstimulated baseline. As the subject is stimulated, you will notice how the clitoral glans increases in size.

With pride, she thought of her breakthrough ideas in the section titled "The Clitoris, One of a Kind," in her most recently published scholarly monograph. But suddenly she felt disconnected, edgy, and the familiar laboratory fell away like a silk scarf from her shoulders.

The clitoris on the chalky screen enlarged, filling the screen completely. Dr. Holl screamed and backed away. The last thing she heard was the pencil tapping the wastebasket, the pencil that she had dislodged while trying to grab the side of the counter on her way to the floor. Physically, she was out cold. Mentally, snippets of the still-running video reached her through her foggy unconscious.

As you can see, vaginal lubrication has not yet begun.

The lab floor did not stop her descent and she continued down, down, down. Below her, the "ground" that she was approaching (or was it coming towards her?) was a huge, fluffy expanse, shaped like South America but more triangular. The downy mound was bigger than many mountains she had seen while flying over the Sierras.

Getting closer to the brown turf, she saw a dark slit in its centre which gave it a benign, furry face. She landed, softly, like a feather pillow, on the hairy terrain to the left of the slit.

No doubt about it. Dr. Holl recognized a mons when she landed on one – and this was a huge one indeed. Like falling right into one of my illustrated anatomy books, she thought dreamily. At the same time, Dr. Holl's own mons, or what she unscientifically referred to as "down there," stirred. Could she be both scientific observer and subject at the same time? Had she fallen onto her own mons? Impossible! But then nothing was as it should be.

North, south, east, and west all looked alike, causing her to lose her bearings. Impenetrable, bushy undergrowth surrounded her, so dense that it darkened the tropical rainforest she had landed in. The lush underbrush rose up to her shoulders. She was utterly lost in acres and acres of the scrub. Such treacherous terrain! The ground itself was snaky – moist and slippery, the consistency of soapy skin. It was hot and humid – she guessed around ninety-eight degrees. Little droplets of moisture coated each of the fantastic teeming bushes. She breathed in a steamy, ocean-fresh fish smell.

Beads of vaginal secretion first appear as isolated droplets, which flow together and eventually moisten the entire inner sur-
face of the vagina. Early in this phase, the quantities of fluid

may be so small as to be unnoticeable. Later, fluid sometimes flows out of the vagina, moistening the labia and the vaginal opening.

The "slit" consisted of a big outer lip and then another smaller lip inside. They changed to a deep burgundy colour, and rose and expanded right before her eyes. The lips opened to reveal a huge, deep, dark crater. To steady herself, she grabbed one of the furry bushes, surprised by its coarseness. Entranced, she stood at the edge of the crater.

What she was about to witness, an active volcano, had been one of Gloria's life-long dreams. From the crater, a hot, mucous-like substance erupted. A fine mist fogged the atmosphere. She stood dazzled by the sight, but not for long. Not paying attention to the creamy lava that had accumulated all around her, she slipped on it and fell head-first into the open-mouthed vagina.

Is this what my colleagues in the LSD experiments in the sixties experienced, wondered the good doctor as she marveled at the narrowing vaginal barrel, whose walls dripped with increasing condensation. Only a glow-worm light allowed her to see through the otherwise pitch black. She saw rainbow-coloured, diamond-studded mermaids with big Y's embroidered on their satin-covered breasts dancing together, and with, vitreous floaters with big Xs moving like ticker tapes across their mutating shapes. Purple and red veins threaded, and thawing stalactites and stalagmites studded, the tissue that encased her. Milky raindrops the size of silver dollars began to pour out of the sides of the subterranean passage. She felt like she had been swallowed by a huge snake whose body cavity kept contracting. And was that a symphony tuning up in the distance?

As she gasped for breath in the steamy chamber, a tickling began between her legs. She craved to scratch it, but instinctively knew that scratching would stop the sensation. The itchiness drove her mad, while at the same time, she coveted it. How odd! Her body was somehow flirting with itself. Her tumescent breasts ballooned around her so much so that she hardly recognized them, they had grown so large. Her distended nipples – erect, proud, obedient soldiers – stood at attention. The ache of her swollen breasts radiated across her torso. Titillating pinpricks danced in a triangle from breasts to crotch, and crotch to breasts. An invisible hand grabbed her crotch in a tightening, powerful vise. The front of the doctor's body became a playground of susceptibility – tickling, burning, aching, and itching. A pinkish rash, beginning in a necklace around her throat, sprayed the rest of her torso. Though mindless, she wanted, with mathematical certainty, to remain in this state. She became fearless; she became all body, a body of ecstatic cells turning somersaults in space. She began to pant.

> *The vasocongestive reaction during the plateau phase usually progresses to such an extent that the outer third of the vaginal barrel becomes grossly distended with venous blood to form the orgasmic platform.*

The vapor rose and whirled around her, dragging her down, down, into its vortex. Pulled along the dark vaginal barrel, she landed in a carnal cavern that expanded like a tent, in fact, grew to twice its original size. When she looked back at the barrel that she had fallen through, she saw only a sliver of light.

She began to hyperventilate. Her heart palpitated and beat wildly against its cage. It also beat in the hole between her legs, obliterating her body's separation of church and state. Her rash deepened into an oscillating flush that covered her skin like an ornate tablecloth. An irresistible impulse was building inside her, skating to and fro, here and there, helter skelter. Up, up, and away she went in an exquisite frenzy, like an unleashed kite in a wind storm. One, two, three. One, two, three. One, two, three. Why am I counting? she asked herself dumbly. She felt giddy. Reason was a dim memory. She laughed like a hyena.

> *Status orgasmus (43 seconds). Here is a combination electrocardiogram and orgasmic platform recording: Heart rate above 180/min. at peak (severe tachycardia) 25 regularly recurrent platform contractions.*

What happened next made everything else look like child's play. Dr. Holl simultaneously saw and had her first orgasm. All activity inside the red-tissue cave came to a stunning stop, like a still-life, for a second. Next, she found herself as if inside a blender with all the options on at once. The violence of the spastic contractions of the tissue around her tossed her to and fro like flotsam and jetsam. She strove to stay afloat by grabbing the slick walls. The contractions seemed to go on and on and on, but when she looked down at her water-resistant watch, she saw that the entire drama took place in less than thirty seconds. Finally, she was swept away by a series of vibrating quakes, after which the tissue collapsed around her like a popped balloon. It became very dark and still.

Dr. Holl's body encountered a parallel adventure. Carnal sensations as sharp as knives led her around like a dog on a leash while, at the same time, the experience was so abstract and out-of-body that she wondered if it was happening to someone else. Her emotions ran wild. One minute, she cried for every tragedy in the world, and the next she laughed at every joke she had ever heard, not able to distinguish the difference. She was a paddle-ball; a rapped, out-of-control ball shooting into space, a tethered ball forced back by the strung paddle, and a paddle whacked by the ball. She lit up like Times Square, her body a jammed intersection of electrified molecules. Dr. Holl saw the hungriest kitties in the world licking and licking a bowl of milk – she could hear their sandpaper tongues – licking until they were scraping the porcelain right off the bowl.

Finally, she had to give it all up, in the warm rush of a radiating flush down there. Wave upon wave slashed the shore. One after the other after the other. She rode them like an agile surfer; she toppled under the undertow; she almost drowned. And then it all stopped. A few ripples. A quiet pool. An indecisive wave that couldn't get off the ground.

Clitoris returns to normal position within 10-15 seconds; platform disappears; vagina returns to resting size quickly (vaginal lips return to normal; uterus and cervix descend).

Gurgling and gasping for air, the doctor came to consciousness. Tears were in her eyes. Good, satisfied tears. The lab looked like a strange hotel room she had awakened in after a long transatlantic flight. She felt a subtle throbbing down there, warm and gooey, like a big can of shaving cream had exploded in her panties.

We hope that you have enjoyed our video. To order more in our series....

Gloria Holl pushed the rewind button while glancing down at her watch: 6PM. Wow! she thought. I slept through the entire video.

How'd I end up on the laboratory floor? I must be exhausted! But, I've made real progress today. I can't exactly put my finger on it, but.... She put her finger on the replay button.

Daytime and Night

CARELLIN BROOKS

CHIP HAS A JOB putting up prostitutes' numbers in telephone boxes. The cards are everywhere, festooning the West End kiosks with a patchwork of spread thighs and sultry looks. She's already been caught once by the police, who warned her and let her go.

"So what are you doing here?" I said when I first met her. We were in my bar. It was for men but they had hired me, a female, a token gesture I guess. I don't know why. The only women who came in were the ones I knew.

Chip was playing pool, all dangling cigarette and swinging chain. American Boy. I watched for a while, then called her over and passed her a bottle. Fortunately we had no-beer in stock, for men who wanted to look butch and stay straight.

"I was working in San Francisco," she says. "I got laid off." Answering the question without answering it. Upstairs, the shadows of men congregate and separate in the weak light from outside. The randomly spaced screens that hang from the ceiling shield them. The darkness in the fuckroom is a sound in itself, compounded by the men's silence as they buckle at the knees, go down. "You?"

"I'm studying." I look her squarely in the eye, wondering if this passes. It's my standard line, not that it explains anything. Why I'm here, for example. Why any of us are here – the expats, the exiles, the ones whose own countries are left behind. Why we stay, when even the stupidest of us can see that we don't belong and aren't wanted. What keeps us here.

When it's time to go, I step out into the back alley with the bags of bottles. Chip is long gone but the last of the customers remain, outside now, silent in the square. By first light they will be gone, back to bedsits and row houses, alone or in pairs. By tomorrow night they will be back again, ordering up pints of Australian lager, sending nervous glances around the bar. There is something they want here. Something they never get. Something that, for all their searching, they can't quite identify. I sympathize with the men. I know the feeling. I have it myself.

The sky is already fading to a dirty grey by the time I turn up the corner towards my rented flat. The church on the corner, delapidated now with disuse, masses in the gloom. My footsteps echo as I take the bridge over the canal, the brackish water eddying beneath. Tomorrow I will sleep late, wake to afternoon's undifferentiated light, go to the library where I enjoy the game of lining up for books that never come until the next day. It's a ritual dance, the flat clerks, unamused, walking away, the desperate foreign students, voices rising and cracking with the strain of getting the right words, the unlocking ones. Outside, people are eating ice cream on the steps of the British Museum. Sometimes I take a left in the lobby, past the hall of statues, and go and look at the stolen marbles, the ones that came from the Parthenon. They're named, though, not for where they come from, but for the thief. They make an incomplete frieze in a far room; the carved flanks of the horses, luscious and fleshy, strain with effort. Other times I go to the room full of clocks; their ticking, for some reason I don't fully understand, soothes me.

Chip calls me on the weekend. She wants to know what I'm doing. Her boss is taking her out to dinner at the Bangkok House and I'm invited.

I turn up in a silk shantung suit, red shirt, matching lipstick. Madame Jean looks me up and down; I can tell she doesn't like what she sees. She lights another cigarette and leans forward, disregarding the food the waiter sets before her.

"She's so American," she says to me in a strange drawl. "Nothing like the girls here."

Chip is wearing a suit Madame Jean bought for her. With her shaved head and stapled earlobes, she looks vaguely menacing. The scrutiny doesn't seem to bother her.

"Where are you girls going after this?" Madame Jean looks around, signals the waiter for another cocktail. I take the opportunity to discreetly shovel more food onto my plate.

"We thought we'd check out the cemetery," Chip mumbles, her mouth full of food. "At Abney Park." I look over; it's the first I've heard of it. Madame Jean is interested, too.

"Darling, they do lock the gates at night." She pauses delicately. "They don't like your kind in there."

Our kind? I don't ask.

Chip doesn't, either. We talk about other things until it's time to go. Madame Jean watches us with one eyebrow raised.

"Goodbye, darling," she says to me, offering a perfumed cheek. "Lovely to meet you."

We take the bus. It pauses in the square for a rabble of boys to get on, bringing the smoke and smell of the pub with them. The vehicle lurches forward and they sway in the aisle, almost falling over, as they attempt to count up change.

"Fuckin' drunks," Chip says. I look out the window. Lights glow over the Thames, but the promenade is empty. Two fishes hold up each standard. She rustles and takes my hand.

"What are you thinking about?" she says softly.

I want to tell her about what happened here, before both of us came. I'd like to explain about the year of the plague. How the people died, how they fell in the street, not a mark on them. How those who took to the great river, mooring their boats there for all of the terrible year, were spared. How the church on the corner by my house was one of the burying places, mass graves where the dumping was done by night. The plague is kinder now, gentler. It comes so softly and slowly we can almost ignore the fact that it is here, among us. I see it in the face of the thin man who comes to the bar, his eyes. Someone my boss knows is in the hospital again.

"Everybody's got it," he says. He's a small man, taut with muscle, his expression kindly. Once I started crying in the middle of my shift, surprising even myself, and he let me sit for a while, away from the crowds demanding beer. "Except me."

I nod and he goes on, telling me because I'm not one of them. "Sometimes I feel guilty. I'm going to live."

I can't explain any of this to Chip. She's a foreigner, like me. "The police came by the other night," I say instead.

"What did they want?"

"There was supposed to be somebody else living there. Another Canadian." I'd seen the envelopes, in the main hallway, recognizing them by their stamps. I'd thought they were for me until I read the name.

"So?" Chip says, still holding my hand. One of the drunks brushes by in the aisle, muttering something when he sees us. Chip tenses, and I squeeze her hand harder.

"Her family called them. Apparently she'd gone off somewhere, and they were worried."

"Did they find her?" Chip's not really interested. She gazes out into the darkness as the bus makes its way through the narrow streets of the City. Threadneedle Street. Cheapside. The great block of the Bank of England looms in the dark, lit up along its extremities. The office buildings along Liverpool Street are strung with lights; workers move in and out even at this late hour, carrying paper and materials. There's a heavy, dim sound of machinery from behind the partially-rebuilt glass façades.

"She's gone." I nudge her. "Look, it's almost our stop."

We walk up the street to the cemetery in silence. I'm breathless, a little scared. None of it matters, I remind myself, sternly, like a person learning a lesson. We're just passing through. We have nothing to leave behind, not even ourselves.

"In here," Chip says, and there's a dip in the wall, a mound on the other side where we can drop softly onto the earth. The cemetery is deserted, its weeping stone monuments sunk into the earth. Marble women drip in the gloom. We walk to the centre where the ruined church has been fenced off, our heels crunching on the loose gravel.

"Over here," Chip says. Her voice is rougher, somehow, in the soft darkness. She reaches for me, her hands heavy. I will be bruised. I will have the marks. Later. I will remember. I look into her face, go where she leads me.

"Come on," she says, "come on," opening my clothes. Touching me. The night air such a shock. My head falls back. I let her. O.

"Come on," she mumbles again, concentrating, cruel. Forcing it in, what she has for me. Taking me by hips and hands, fitting me like a lid. I make a noise. It's a small one, lost in her shoulder. She grips me. Moments go by when we are each moving, both mechanical, both quiet. Then I stiffen, lift my head.

"Did you hear that?" I say.

"What?" she whispers back.

I look behind me, towards the paths that gird the cemetery, and I see him. It's a man, flat-capped, serenely pedalling a bicycle. His back is straight; he doesn't turn around to look at us, our wet breath against the cold stone.

"Did you see that?" I ask her. "Did you see that man?"

"I saw ... something," she says. She gazes at me, wondering.

We dress and go out again, over the wall. On the street, people pass by, calling to each other. One of the pubs is still open, and a restaurant too brightly lit for comfort.

It's a few weeks later, on the bus again, when I punch her lightly in the arm. "Do you remember the doorway?"

"Yes," she says. It was the night after the cemetery. She was walking me to work, to the old pub where the walls, upstairs, crumbled in your hands. The sound of ricocheting bathroom doors in the basement disco sharp as gunshots as the men slammed in, then out again. We were crossing the canal on the way there. There was a door, ajar, and a row of electricity meters in the dark. Dust. She knelt down. I leaned against the wall. The door a thin gap between us and the rest of the world.

Afterwards we stumbled out. Her mouth smeared when I kissed her. "I keep looking," I say now. "But I can't find it any more. Can you?"

She shakes her head and we look at each other. Wondering.

We get off the bus at Liverpool Street and walk over to the pub in the station forecourt. Workers in suits skirt us, heading for offices or shops. The ceilings here are painted with cherubs and garlands, a bright sky-blue; the outside tables gleam chrome.

Liam is sitting at one of them, wearing an orange shirt. He rolls his eyes when I ask him about work.

"Let's not talk about it," he says. "You know what this place used to be?"

We shake our heads. "The main reception room of the hospital," Liam continues. "You can see the arches." He points back into the pub, to the cherubed ceiling. "They'd bring the relatives in, convince them how great it was." He closes his eyes briefly, drinks from his pint. "Bedlam," he says.

Later he'll show us the single plaque with its dates, set around the corner from the little hotel. In the days to come, when we're back at the station, we'll buy rock cakes at the bakery and hurry through to our trains, dispelling the ghosts with our furious steps. Liam doesn't ask how long we're here for. Nobody can answer that question and he knows it.

"So what have you two been up to?" he asks when we bring back our beer, and I find myself telling him, without planning to, about the ghost.

"It was only that he seemed so ordinary, riding that bicycle," I say, trying to explain. Sitting there in the warm sunlight, drinking beer. "It was only that he looked so much like he was going some- where, when we both knew there was nowhere for him to go."

She Was a Mountain of a Woman

ERIN GRAHAM

WHEN LORETTA WALKED INTO THE GYM, I knew something had happened. I could feel her. I could smell her. The hair on the back of my neck stood up. I turned around, and there she was, the most splendid example of a powerlifting icon I have ever laid eyes on. She stood 6'2" and she weighed 225 pounds if she weighed an ounce (that's 100 kilograms, but 225 sounds so much more impressive). She had no neck to speak of, her trapezius muscles went from the base of her ears to her deltoids, and she had the most arresting grey eyes I have ever fallen into.

She came over to the storage closet that was to be the weigh-in room. Standing this close to her, I could smell her perfume. White Shoulders or something. I noticed she wore make-up. Blue eyeshadow yet. Her dark hair was curly like mine, but longer. She had full lips, the colour of, I believe, dusty rose. Her breath smelled of caffeine and peppermints. The woman was 100 kilograms of pure muscular trailer park trash and I was in love.

I was ready for the weigh-in; registration forms and rulebook out on the table, the scales calibrated. It was 8:30AM and the competitors for the Women's Provincial and Men's Open Powerlifting meet were just beginning to arrive. They were warming up at the squat racks, arranging their belts, shoes, squat suits, bench shirts, and wraps for the equipment check; and telling each other lies about lifts they had made in the gym. The platform was set up, barbells and plates at the ready.

By this time it was getting pretty noisy in the gym. But in that moment, all the clanging of iron plates against one another, the soft grunts of people warming up and the murmurs of conversation fell away. The smell of iron and chalk was wafted over by something else. Pheromones, I guessed. Mine. Roaring hell-bent for hers.

"Hi," she said, "my name's Loretta. When do you want me?"

"Want you?" I blushed. How could she have known what I was thinking?

"For weigh-in and all that. What time should I be here?" She looked at me with those grey eyes, innocent of my discomfort.

There were four other women competing and as they were all considerably lighter than she, they got on the scales first. They would also give me their first attempts for each of the three lifts. It's a pretty straightforward procedure. I told her another twenty minutes.

That twenty minutes became forty-five, because none of the other women had bothered to write down or memorize their opening attempts. There seemed no end to the fuss. "Oh, my boyfriend has it, just a minute...." or "My coach is late and he has them all figured out...." or " Uh, what is that in kilograms again?"

Every second of "Where is (insert boyfriend's name) with my numbers?" was a second longer I would have to wait to see Loretta in her underwear. I kept seeing her traps rising out of the collar of her t-shirt. What pectorals that girl must have! It was all I could do to keep from snapping at the other women, "You're fucking boyfriend isn't lifting, is he? These are *your* openers, *you* tell me!"

Finally her time came. She came into the weigh-in room. She was very big. The room was very small. I came about level with her breastbone.

"Hi," she said, "Loretta."

"I remember. I'm Sam," I said. Sam is short for Sandra. "Nice to meet you." We shook hands. We both had calluses from lifting. Her hand felt wonderful in mine. Nice grip.

"Do you want my opening lifts now, or after I weigh in?"

Damn, I thought, finally, we're alone in this room, and she has to be so efficient she'll be out of here in no time. "Doesn't matter, really." I stammered. My knees trembled. Oh dear. I was a quivering mass of nerves and pumping glands. I looked down at my shoes.

"Are you ready?" she said.

"For what?" I whispered.

"My openers." She looked at me as if I had a third eye in the middle of my forehead. I wished I did, I could see more of her.

I cleared my throat, flushed. "Of course." I grabbed a pen and her registration card. "Squat?"

"155 kilos." I wrote it in the appropriate box. 341 pounds.

"Bench?" I wiped my right palm against my pant leg, held the pen more tightly.

"Ninety-five kilos." She smiled at me. "I'm not as strong in the bench press."

"Not many of us are," I said. "Ninety-five is a pretty good start, I'd say. What are you hoping for?"

"If I get 120 kilos, I'll be happy. I had a rotator cuff problem a few months ago, I don't want to push it."

Don't want to push it. I don't think I will *ever* press 100 kilograms. Mind you, it's unlikely I will ever weigh that, either. Were her nerve endings standing up and scraping the inside of her skin the way mine were?

"Want my deadlift?" she asked. I cleared my throat, nodded.

"I'm going to start with 175 today," she said, "I feel pretty good."

"Uh-huh. Openers, hey?" I was impressed.

"Honey, I weigh ninety-eight kilograms. I think I can open with these," she smiled.

Honey. She called me "honey." I grinned at her. "Step on the scales, Loretta, let's see if you speak the truth."

She peeled her shirt off over her head. She wasn't wearing a bra. Then she removed her warm-up pants. She wore a thong. It was black and edged with lace. I had never seen anyone so magnificent as Loretta Sweeney in nothing but her very tiny underwear. Her pecs were, as I expected, something to behold. They swelled from her collarbone, perfect and strong. Her legs looked nearly as big around as my waist, and solid, too. When she moved, everything rippled, including the air between us.

She stepped onto the scales. I moved my hand to adjust the weights and bumped her forearm. I apologized and looked up at her. She was looking at me, too. My stomach skidded into my heart. "Don't worry about it," she said, smiling.

Then I noticed her left hand. She wore a ring on the third finger. An amethyst in a gold setting. My face flushed, I felt a little nauseous. "Your boyfriend coming today?" I asked as she dressed.

"Boyfriend?" she asked, then laughed. "Oh, the ring. Honey, I just wear that to warn the jokers off." This information was a very good sign.

I laughed with her, much relieved, wished her luck, and secretly, myself as well. The rest of the morning sped by. There was

113

equipment to check and the rack heights for the squat to set for each lifter. The athletes, loaders, and spotters needed to be briefed.

––––––––

This was my first time refereeing a powerlifting meet on my turf, Commercial Drive, Vancouver's "Dyke Central." You'd think that a sport involving so much black iron, sweat, and unattractive costuming would attract lesbians by the truckload. But no. I am usually the only one. It was nice this time to be at Spartacus Gym in the heart of the Drive. The audience was full of lesbians. Young women sporting tattoos and multi-coloured hair; middle-aged warriors wearing tee shirts with the sleeves rolled over cigarette packages; spiky-haired leather dykes and a few lipstick lesbians peppered the crowd, mingling with the bikers and muscleheads who regularly came to these things. All of the lifters (except Loretta, another good sign) seemed a little nervous about the queer contingent, but accepted their presence with good humour overall. The female lifters eventually let go of their fear of being hit on by any "ooga-booga lesbian" and enjoyed the attention. It was a great crowd; they hooted and cheered and stomped their feet. It wasn't long into the lifting that it became apparent Loretta was the crowd favourite, as well as mine.

––––––––

The squat is the most arresting of the powerlifts, more elegant than any gymnastic flip or balletic twirl. It is simply a deep knee bend with a barbell held on the shoulders. Barbell and lifter become one. A proper squat is done with legs shoulder width or wider apart, back straight, chest up, and hips directly below the shoulders. The back is straight and the lifter's gaze never wavers from the spot at the back wall where it meets the ceiling. The lifter squats, knees travel over the toes, heels remain on the floor, and the tops of the thighs go down so they are just below parallel with the hips. Then there is the thrust of buttocks and hips and abdominal muscles to stand. It's a powerful move, full of danger and grace.

Most lifters wear squat suits. Tiny little garments made of something like a million little bungee cords sewed together with elastic bands. Takes two people to put it on, if it fits right, and in them most people look like a sausage escaping its casing. Especially women. The suits are not designed to accommodate breasts and hips.

Loretta, however, looked marvelous in hers. It emphasized the enormous yet lean circumference of her legs, and she looked like a corseted super-hero. I was head ref for the squat, which meant I gave the signals to start the lift and then to rack the weight upon completion. Loretta took the bar upon her shoulders; looked at me to signal she was ready, and *winked* at me. I sucked in my breath, my cunt contracted. My arm swept down, I said, "Start." She dropped down, her butt nearly touched her heels, and then she rose as if her legs were hydraulic pistons. At the top of the lift, she thrust her hips forward and I nearly fell back on my chair. We stared at one another. Her dusky rose lips were glistening, and so, I was sure, were both sets of mine. I started to rise from my chair to go toward her when she cleared her throat.

"Uh, Sam, can I put it down now?" she grunted at me.

"Oh! Yeah! Rack it, rack it!" I said and motioned with my arm to signal the spotters to help her back to the rack. The other two referees, both men, looked at me from their seats at either side of the platform and snickered. The crowd of watchers behind me tittered. "Okay,okay," I muttered. "Sorry, Loretta."

"Focus, coach," she said with a grin.

I *was* focussed. Just, at that moment, on something other than powerlifting. I gave her a green light. So did the other referees. A good lift.

———

While the lifters were warming up for the bench press, I ran upstairs to grab a coffee from the Café Roma above the gym. To the north, down the Drive, Grouse Mountain loomed above the city. There was snow already, glimmering in the low sun of fall. I looked up at the mountain and thought of Loretta's traps again. I sighed. A couple of women walked by me, all green hair and piercings, leaning into one another, laughing at some shared joke. They looked sideways at me in my blazer and grey pants. I smiled at them and returned to the gym, coffee in hand.

———

The bench press went quickly. Loretta took her position. She planted her feet into the floor, arched her back steeply, nestled her shoulders onto the bench, and tucked her chin into her chest, gazing directly up at the bar. She was like a spring-tight coil. Only her ass and her shoulders were on the bench; she looked like she had been welded there. The bar was loaded with 120 kilos. Her third attempt. The audience hushed. I gave her the signal to start. I looked at the arch in her back and imagined her doing the same motion for a different reason, imagined my tongue between her legs and my hands moving along her ribcage towards her breasts, her nipples, her collarbone. I imagined nibbling at her earlobes, smelling her perfume and her sweat. I imagined tasting her neck, feeling her arch toward me and put her mouth to mine. I *saw* her press the weight smoothly off her chest and lock her arms out, but I was so involved in imagining I forgot to flick the switch on my light box. I heard the crowd shifting, and Loretta broke my reverie by saying, "Um, Sam, what do you think, red or green?"

"Aw shit," I mumbled, flicked the switch, green light.

The spectators were delighted. They cheered and whistled, called her name.

"Lor-ETT-A, Lor-ETT-A!" they hollered. She swept up from the bench and waved at her admirers, grinning ear to ear.

"Thanks, buddy," she said, and sashayed off to the warm up pit again. It isn't easy to sashay in a wrestling singlet and a bench shirt, but she managed. She was going six for six so far. Another break, then onto the deadlift. I resolved to haul my brain cells back north and think of nothing but powerlifting for the rest of the day.

————

The deadlift is the lift where the most iron can be moved. The lifter bends to a barbell on the floor and stands up with it. No jerking, no heaving it over the head, just standing up. A simple and impressive lift. Loretta was starting with 175 kilograms, or 385 pounds. She lowered herself to the floor, grasped the bar, looked up and rose. A mountain of a woman, holding that barbell as if it were a broomstick. Oh my.

Her final attempt was 250 kilograms – 550 pounds. I had never seen a woman lift a quarter of a ton. The crowd hushed as Loretta chalked her hands. She was supremely focussed. She stepped up to the bar, placed her feet wide beneath it, bent her knees and reached for the bar. Her head went up, she gathered herself and pushed her feet into the floor, brought her hips beneath her torso, the bar rose … and stopped. The weight stayed hovering at her shins. She tried to straighten, tried to roll her shoulders up, but it was too much. The crowd yelled, "C'mon, Loretta! It's yours, you can do it!" The other lifters were into it too, screaming, "Pull, pull Loretta. It's yours, sister!" I held my breath and strained with her.

Our eyes met; we inhaled at the same time. She brought her chest up, her back straightened and she brought the weight the rest of the way, rolling her shoulders back. Beautiful lift, just beautiful. I gave the signal, "Down."

The gym exploded. Loretta leapt up, pumping both hands above her head. I opened my arms to her. She ran to me and picked me up. The crowd hooted and stomped their feet, the other lifters pounded her on the back as she whirled around the platform with me in her muscular arms. That little victory dance seemed to last forever. The lights of the gym flashed around me. The sound of the people and the smell of chalk dust, iron and her sweat blended to an ambience of passion. She kissed me on both cheeks, put me down, looked into my eyes and cupped my chin in her hand.

"Thanks, Sam." She said, "I love this sport."

"Uh-huh," I breathed. "Me too."

Going Down Under

DEAN DURBER

OUR TEN-DAY TRIP was drawing to a close. Soon the heat of Sydney would fall far into the distance, replaced by the sudden winter chill of a bleak London sky. I couldn't wait. This sun had scorched my face. Mosquitoes, cockroaches, spiders, they had plagued my hotel room from the day we had arrived in the hope of glory.

"Let's kick some Aussie arse," we had yelled, waving to friends and family we promised to fill with pride. Eight matches later – seven lost, one drawn – we were hanging our heads in shame.

———

Our coach must have thought a trip to Sydney's most famous landmark could help to brighten our dampened spirits. He thought wrong. Who cared about the history of a building that was nothing but concrete and dirty white tiles? Did any one of us give a shit about some sad old Danish architect who had never seen his dream come true? We had but one mission in mind – a team effort – to make the guide look stupid by talking amongst ourselves, refusing to listen, asking unrelated questions impossible to answer, and treating him like the man he was, like an Aussie, putting him in his place. This victory was ours.

"That's a big organ you've got there, mate!"

We roared with laughter, filling the vastness of the Concert Hall with the up-front, unashamed filth of our rugby-boy culture. It was natural for us to find smut in anything. We had single-handedly defined the word.

"Yes, it is," answered the guide, calmly, passing his eyes to every one of us, as if he somehow enjoyed the challenge. "It happens to be the biggest organ in the world, but then, who's bragging?"

We laughed again.

"Unfortunately," he continued, "I rarely get a chance to use it."

We sighed, and pitied his honesty.

"Let me have a go on it then," I said. "I'll get it working for you."

The guide now looked at me, and me alone, as my comrades supported my quip with deep cheers, disturbing once again the harmony of that hall. Yeah, good one, son, you give him a hand.

"We'll see to that later," whispered the guide. "But I warn you, mate, you may find this one a bit too much to handle."

He had me blushing red.

———

A few photos later – forbidden inside, but taken anyway when the guide wasn't looking – and our tour was done. We trampled noisily down the steps, refusing to acknowledge the respect this building deserved. What was it, anyway? Nothing more than the symbol of a land we hated. Nothing to do with us. Though I noticed a few of my buddies shaking the guide's hand, thanking him for his humour, forgetting that he was one more Aussie who had defeated our attempts at humiliation. And I felt myself strangely drawn to offer the same.

"You're quite funny. For an Aussie."

I took his hand and stared nervously into his face.

"And you're quite friendly. For a pomme."

His eyes were confidently fixed on mine. And for a moment, a flash of rugby filled my mind. I wondered if he had ever played. Did he like getting dirty on the field?

"Did you enjoy it?"

I was dazed.

"Did you enjoy the tour?"

I nodded.

"There's more to see. If you want."

I tried to shake my head. I had seen enough. Really. And besides, there wasn't time. We had to go.

"Make sure you are all back on the bus in half an hour!" screamed the coach, as fourteen members of my team raced to toilets, shops, and outdoor smoking zones. Okay, so I had some time, and besides, my hand was still linked to his.

———

On the other side of the building, the Opera Theatre was dark. The ceilings were painted all black, swallowing up what little light filtered from the stage. I had been comfortable in the brightness of the Concert Hall, with my friends; not alone with this man and the sight of those few male dancers prancing about on stage. Black ballet tights clinging to muscular legs. The tightness of their stomachs. I was fascinated.

"Have you ever been to see a ballet?"

I shook my head more often than I needed to. Me? Go to see a ballet? What for?

"There's one on tonight, if you like."

"I can't," I whispered, afraid now that my voice might carry throughout the theatre. "We're flying home tomorrow. Early in the morning. Otherwise I would love to."

I had never once entertained the idea. Come on, lads, night out at the ballet. Thin little girls with skirts right up to their cracks and fags in leotards with fake bulges at the front. My team would have laughed.

"Tomorrow, you say. That's a shame."

Ballet was not for the likes of me. I played rugby. Rough stuff. For boys.

"My girlfriend would love this," I rushed to say just as quickly as a sudden jerk of my leg, or his, brought our knees banging together.

"Your girlfriend?"

"Yeah, my girlfriend. She would love this, my girlfriend would."

The contact between us remained.

———

One by one the ballet dancers flitted out to the wings, and suddenly they were gone. I sat with my guide in an empty theatre and waited for him to speak. He said nothing. What time was it? The bus would be waiting. I was holding everybody up. I needed the toilet. Not the touch of that hand on my leg and the gentle stroke of those fingers moving towards a straining bulge that had formed with rapid ease inside my jeans, tightly locked away until he slipped inside the gaps between the buttons, flicking them open one by one. I rested my head on the back of the seat as he leaned into my lap and started to kiss the rugby-boy sweat of my pants, displaying the warmth of his lips, the softness and moistness of his tongue, tickling the spout of my exposed cock, where drips of come had already begun to leak.

"You like ballet dancers."

121

Was it a question? I groaned. An uncontrollable spasm.

"Your thick hairy legs pinning their slender weakness down to the ground."

His hand struggled to force its way between the seat and my arse. I wanted to resist. I placed my hands on either side and used the muscles in my arms to raise myself one inch higher, allowing him room to fumble for wispy hairs beyond my balls.

"What is it you want to do to those ballet dancers?"

I mumbled.

"What is it you think of when you see their fragile bodies there on stage? Tell me."

"I want to fuck 'em."

This wasn't me. I would never have said that. The boys on the bus, they mustn't hear. They must never know what is happening. Was it still dark out there? Could anybody see?

"What?"

"Fuck 'em. Fuck 'em."

I saw it all. Lying there on the stage, the lights burning down on my skin, scorching my face, with an audience that gasped in anticipation. I held the boy down under the weight of my body and began to tear a tiny hole through the rear of his tights. My cock was hard, resting in my hand, pressing against him. I was ready to do it until the sudden thrust of a finger inside me forced my eyes wide open.

"Wanna fuck them, do you?"

No. That wasn't it. Now I wanted to cry. I could hear the echo of sobs as I told him, yes, I wanted to fuck them all, and started to bounce my body up and down in time with the rapid increase of his finger movements. My hairy arse, naked on the seat, getting fucked by this man, just a guide, just an Aussie, one day before I would fly home to my girl who would never do this to me, could never do this to me. I needed more time. Ten days, all gone too fast. I begged him to keep going, to let me stay longer, clinging on with desperation to his hand beneath me, smacking his palm hard against my naked skin until I exploded and saw signs of come dripping down the face of a man on his knees, and heard groans from my lips reverberate throughout the entire space of that blackness. English-boy sperm had made its mark. This was a victory at last.

———

"What have you been up to?" asked an inquisitive mate as I stepped on the bus, my face all flushed and worried that they might know. Soon, the white sails of Sydney's icon would float alone far in the distance.

"Nothing much. The usual. Just giving the Aussies what for."

I closed my eyes and tried to sleep.

"Yeah. Good one, mate. Two fingers to the Aussies."

My mates cheered, relishing and prolonging the insult, while I shuffled and wondered what two fingers would be like.

Sukreswara

KRISTINE HAWES

I STEPPED FORWARD as the woman in front of me moved ahead. I was firmly planted in the middle of a human chain, linked from the doorway of the temple to the riverbank. The people around me were clothed in bright white cottons, intricate silks, and brilliant flowers. The scents of creamy jasmine and dense orange poppies mingled with the pungent aromas of cinnamon, cardamom, tea, and nutmeg. The dark chocolate faces around me contrasted with their vivid necklaces of colour. Offering bowls filled with ripe fruits and small metal trinkets sat beside their owners, some also sitting as they waited their turn to seek some solace in their god.

I didn't know if I believed or not. Puttabhi believed. Maybe that was all that was necessary. I looked down at my caramel-coloured hands, gold bracelets on my wrists. He'd given me everything I desired. He took care of me as every man of his upbringing would – with fine, golden things, a lush home, a traditional Indian family to care for me. Everything that seemed lacking in my transparent, American-tinged upbringing. Everything except a child.

The line moved ahead slowly as another woman slipped into the sheath of the dark doorway. The humid sun hung above the tiled rooftops. I raised my veil to cover my unaccustomed skin and sighed. Puttabhi said it was my duty to serve Him, to please Him; only then would the child be brought to us. Puttabhi was raised here, his belief had grown as he had; it had become part of his very skin. I grew up only hearing stories of India, not really believing there was such a place where the gods spoke to you. Gods didn't speak to us in America. It was too noisy for us to hear. But Puttabhi believed. We packed our bags and flew from California to Delhi, travelled into the depths of the Assam Valley, to Assam, where His river, the

Brahmapurta, begins. Go, Puttabhi said as I stood at the gates of the massive temple. Go make your offerings. Make them until our child is secure.

Every day, many people would cross the rivers to make their offerings in the twin temples. Hers, Durga's, was filled with the old and young, men and women, hoping for Her to give them new life; some token to help them succeed in their lives. Shiva's temple was different. Women stood and sat, hundreds, waiting for their turn to touch, to taste, to breathe in His aura for the briefest of moments. To take with them the essence of His manhood, His seed. This was my first time. I looked down at my slightly shaking hands and wrung them. I was Puttabhi's wife; I had to believe him, even if I did not believe myself. I picked up my wooden bowl of oranges and shifted one person closer to the entrance.

The women around me ignored me. My foreignness clothed me, no matter what my face looked like. They spoke in hushed tones amongst themselves, their soft murmur nearly incomprehensible to me. I closed my eyes, let my body absorb the heat. Twenty more and I would be inside. It must be before the sun set, I thought, I could not stand waiting all day for nothing.

I watched the neophytes walk regally though the courtyard and buildings. Here, men cared for Shiva and Durga. The men were silent and efficient, their shaved heads bobbing as they moved through the crowd. With arms embedded in heaps of limp poppies, roses, and spice branches, they made their way to the inner temples. I caught their eyes; a light-skinned woman was a wonder in this part of the world. Some were curious and stared. Others shunned me as a disbeliever. Maybe they could see inside of me where I could not. They all continued on their way, my face and meaning fading in light of their tasks. Another man carried a small box filled with pieces of paper and small icons. The priests would take these names, make offerings of incense and song. This was not religion, no. It was a state of being. I envied them their belief.

———

Closer. The decaying stone cast a cool radiation around the entrance. I let my veil fall and revelled in the abundant shade. I could smell dying moss and living flesh, but could see nothing. My stomach constricted around my spine. What would I ask of Him? What would they ask me to do? From the darkness I heard move-

ment, shuffling, footsteps. A woman covered her face as she left the
shrine and descended the stone stairs. I followed her movements,
wishing I could follow her. If I did, what would I tell Puttabhi? I
turned toward the doors. A young priest beckoned me with his
hands. He did not speak because he knew I would not understand.
I betrayed my fear and followed.

The darkness cradled me with cupped hands. I walked slowly
until my eyes adjusted to the dimness. The hallway before me was
cool, dark. A soft hand clasped my wrist and tugged me forward. I
could see the man smiling. It was all right, he was telling me. Do not
be afraid. We turned several times and the darkness deepened. I
could hear chanting, soft sounds in the distance. We turned once
more, into an alcove, through a doorway.

I could not walk further. There, in the centre of a raised dais,
stood a glistening stone man, poised, ready to strike down. Not
merely a man. A god. Shiva, the Destroyer. His feet were planted
firmly on the polished floor, a ready display of power and strength.
Delicate chains and bells were carved into the ankles of the god's
smooth legs. The orange, yellow, and gold from the heaped offerings
reflected in the milky white skin of the god, sheathing His legs in an
illusion of flames. His hips tapered into a narrow waist, almost feminine, encircled with a carved, gem-inlaid belt. Stomach, ribs, chest –
intricately chiselled and smoothed – flowed from his waist upward,
into rounded, smooth shoulders. His arms ascended in a graceful
arc toward the ceiling. His dancing hands, thick and oversized,
clasped the rays of light that shot down from the broken-tiled roof.
His smooth, placid face looked down upon me. His eyes set with
huge rubies, His lips full and round, His cheeks and nose angled and
lustrous. Serene. Complete. He stood glorious and naked before me.
My eyes descended the god's body. Naked, yes, and full of life. His
lingam stood straight and proud: explicit, long, and surrounded at
the base with wreathes of purple and red flowers. A flash of heat
coated my cheeks and breast. I looked down quickly. Bowls of red
ochre lined the floor at the god's feet – bowls of bloody soup.

My guide smiled at my wonder and embarrassment. He said
nothing as he touched my elbow and pointed to the dais. He
motioned with his hands – go, give what you have. I lifted my sari
and ascended the small steps. My offering was one of hundreds. I
looked up. The weight of the god pulled me forward.

I knelt, as Puttabhi had told me, placed my bowl to one side of

Shiva's feet. I bowed low, pressed my forehead to the cool grey tile, and leaned back. Shiva's lingam stood out above my head, within reach. This close, its length was daunting. I was both fascinated and frightened. *This* was what all women came to give their offerings to; not only to the god but also to the power He provided. Intense, sexual power. My fingers unwound from the fabric of my dress and slowly rose. I stopped, looked back over my shoulder. The priest stood quietly, his hands folded, his eyes unmoving. He nodded once. I turned and let my hand continue.

The opaque lingam was cool, cooler than the floor on which I knelt. My fingers brushed the rounded head, tracing the deeply carved line of its ridge. My fingers circled the shaft and my palm flattened as I stroked downward. The glossy spear was polished with soft hollows and minute rises. Desire grew inside my breast. My body grew warm and my own sex ached. My hand flowed down the shaft until it descended into the fragrant flowers at the base. I raised my other hand and together, hands clasped, I caressed upward, feeling the strength of His erection filling me.

A body, warm and startling, pressed against me from behind. My nerves jolted but I did not stop. Dark hands covered mine as I stroked the god's solid member. Saffron, sweat, and unwashed cotton – scents assaulted me as I tried to keep my focus. My guide's hands slowed, stopped. I didn't know what to do, where to go. I looked over my shoulder. The man's mahogany eyes calmed me. He smiled, his teeth gleaming against dusky, mellow skin. I rocked backward and rested on my heels. He continued holding my hand, pulled gently, and helped me up. His hands were firm and slow as they turned me toward him. I looked past him, ashamed of what I had done to the statue. I realized then that there were two other priests in the dark corners of the room. Watchers. Silent. My embarrassment grew. I looked to the floor.

The priest's fingers touched my chin and gently raised it upward. His eyes were clear, deep. They held mine steadily as his hands moved downward, resting on my hips. He did not smile. His fingers worked slowly, pulling my sari upward. The cool air, humid as it was, chilled my now-bare legs. My breath came in gasps. My sex ached and my heart beat loudly. I could not move. Puttabhi had said nothing of this. Perhaps he did not know. He only trusted in Shiva. I shoved my fear into Puttabhi's trust and held it there.

I wanted to stop the priest's hands, but the tension in his eyes held me. My hands would not move to stop him, my eyes continued to rest on his. He did not speak to me but I understood. My cheeks flushed. I didn't know if I could. His hands stopped moving, the patterned silk bunched up in the palms of his hands. My legs were completely bare, the skin of my back and buttocks sticky with drying sweat. Cool, dark air moved around me. Still, the priest held my eyes. His hands pushed lightly against my hipbones, pushing me backward. I began panting. What if someone saw me? The priests! What if I should not do this? Was this right? My feet did not want to move.

The priest felt my hesitation. He whispered something in a very soft voice. I only understood the word "offering." I had heard it so much while waiting in line. His voice echoed in the dark chamber. I could hear the movements of others within the temple. Would they pass by this room and know? Was this normal? He spoke again, the same words, gently, comforting. I closed my eyes and swallowed and took a step backward.

Within two steps I felt the statue behind me. The carved tower of milky white and shadow-dark stone covered me. I was the lover swallowed. Shiva's lingam pressed against my buttocks. I opened my eyes and looked again at the man who guided me here. I placed my hands on his, holding my sari, and I clasped the fabric tightly. The priest let me go as my body connected with the statue. He took a step backward and knelt. I looked down on him, my heart full of fear. He nodded, passing me a look of serenity. I moved back. I was too short. I closed my eyes and raised up on the balls of my feet. The polished stone felt cool. The head of the statue's lingam pressed against the lips of my yoni, taking my heat quickly. I tilted my hips backward, spread my legs slightly, and surrendered to the will of Shiva.

My body opened to the strength of the stone god. I kept my eyes closed and concentrated on letting His erection fill my body. My wetness covered the head of the lingam, making the crystal slick. I pushed backward, swaying slightly as my yoni opened wider. My spine tingled and heat brushed against my thighs. Sweat coated the back of my knees and my palms holding cool silk. I rocked forward, then back, moving more of the god's lingam into my swollen sex. I let go of the terror, fell into my breath and heartbeat. I opened my eyes, half-lidded, and looked down on the priest. His mouth moved, quiet words obliterated by my heavy breathing. His eyes glittered, hands pressed together in supplication.

I imagined the god's hands, thick and wide, resting upon me, holding me as I impaled myself on Him. Puttabhi, oh, Puttabhi never had this strength. The strength to cause me to yield. I rocked forward and back, my moans filling the stone chamber. The priest also rocked, in time with me, his chants becoming louder. I could not see the other priests so well; lust had darkened my sight. My knees grew weak, blood rushed through me. Closer I came to the edge. My hands tightened around bunched silk. I wanted to feel the god's sex become huge inside me, swelling and opening me, His seed filling me. I let my head fall, my long, black hair swaying with my movements. Back. Forth. The stone was hot fire burning through me. The priest's chanting grew louder, pulsing in time with my movements. I pushed and pulled, forcing the lingam against my womb, my cries in concert with every connection. It was enough. I shuddered and let the climax fill my body. I let out a loud moan, head back, shuddering in each narrow wave of pleasure.

The darkness in my eyes was gone. My head rolled forward, covered with sweat. I could not move. Breathing, simply breathing, peaceful. Warmth came to me, stood in front of me. The priest. My guide. I could not look at him. His arms surrounded me, guided my release from the statue. I nearly fell as the smooth crystal emerged from my still-shaking yoni, my knees too weak to hold my body upright. My breath slowed, my heart returned to its place in my breast. I let my sari fall, once again the proper woman. The priest guided me to the edge of the dais and we turned.

The god stood as before, burnt blood eyes glistening in the twilight, proud body rising to the heavens. We both knelt, bowed to the floor. Acknowledging the offering of self. I leaned back and looked up. My sex was warm, flowing, satisfied. The god looked peaceful. Steadfast. I looked over at the priest who simply nodded. He whispered lyrical words. Shiva. Pleasure. I did not know. Puttabhi would be waiting for me at the gates. He would be looking to me for the token of his god's pleasure. Our god's pleasure. I hoped I would be able to give it to him.

Symphony

STEVE NUGENT

It was my third night in Berlin. The preceding days had been spent recovering from nights in the clubs along the Kleistrasse, so I thought that an evening with the Berlin Symphony Orchestra might slow my pace a little.

A bitter rain drove me from the U-Bahn, across the Gendarmenmarkt, and into the Konzerthaus. The formally dressed crowd in the lobby seemed to part, as if avoiding me, as I carefully made my way through them in dripping wind cheater and Nikes. Once in the theatre I wriggled out of my shoes and jacket and pushed them under the seat. I looked around me, awed by the beauty of the interior. The main work on the programme was Mahler's *Ninth Symphony*.

Reading the programme distracted me until I became aware that the mounting discord of the orchestra tune-up had reached its climax, and that the orchestra members were patiently waiting for the conductor. To scattered applause, he walked quickly to the podium and raised his baton.

My gaze automatically ran across the orchestra members – but it never got past the first violist.

His hair, like ebony under the strong lighting, was swept back from his olive-skinned face. Dark, deep-set eyes reflected his intense concentration as he played, flicking a glance, now and then, at the conductor. His full lips were slightly parted, and occasionally he would slowly draw his tongue across the lower lip, moistening it. Every movement was smooth and confident; he seemed to use his entire body as he swept the bow across his instrument, keeping his legs well apart, one foot ahead of the other.

I couldn't loosen my gaze. It wasn't just his physical appearance that aroused me; it was his complete involvement in what he was doing, his dedication. Everything else seemed apart from him. That excited me, for I had always wanted to commit deeply to what I was doing, but could never seem to stretch beyond a series of transient enthusiasms.

At the end of the movement, he let his bow dangle from his hand, resting across his thigh which showed its strongly muscled line through his black pants. His mound was clearly outlined between his parted legs. I then realized how my cock was responding, hardening, and pushing against my jeans. I thought of how powerful and passionate he would be in making love – that earnestness, that strength, that commitment.

When he met my gaze, I was unprepared for him. Just before positioning his bow he looked directly at me, and then quickly away. Had he really glanced at me? It became the game of to and fro that I so often played out in bars or cafés. There was a glance, and then another, between periods of playing. His expression stayed unchanged. I became more excited, thrilled by possibilities.

The music swirled about me, the warm, lyrical strength of the adagio seemed intent on absorbing me into its intensity and sensuality, accentuating my feelings of desire and longing for the violist. I realized then that I was powerless to move my concentration away from him. Obsessively attending to his every move, my vision narrowing, I thought of how I might take the viola and bow from him, laying them aside as he, initially surprised but unprotesting, would draw me to him, his yielding body pressing against me in anticipation. I gently kiss him, at first savouring the softness of his lips and then searching his mouth with my tongue, as he quickly surrenders to my fantasy of possession.

I lost my sense of time, having no idea how long my imagination had connected him to me until I began to realise that the eerie stillness of Mahler's music was drawing me back to consciousness of my surroundings.

The violist was performing with that same intense expression. The symphony was drawing to a close. My cock was softening.

The audience's applause grew as the conductor brought the orchestra to its feet. The violist, instrument and bow hanging by his side, stood, somewhat shyly acknowledging the approval. When released by the conductor, he quickly left the stage.

I found the stage door and positioned myself to observe him as he came out. He was with a colleague, and I was certain that he had looked around as if searching for someone. I slowly crossed the Platz, going towards him so that I would be in his full view. He saw me from about ten paces. Quickly turning away while searching his pockets, I could hear him excuse himself from his colleague with a brisk "Gute Nacht." He then went back through the stagedoor. I wondered if he was attempting to avoid me, and then hoped that he might be using a ruse to shake off his colleague. My feet were cold and wet, and as the crowd thinned and moved away from the Konzerthaus, I questioned what I was doing. If he had no interest in me, I felt I was playing the role of a stalker. Perhaps best to get out and leave the situation.

I was about to leave when he came out again. Before I could react, he stood facing me. He smiled and said, "I expect you are trying to, what is known in English as, 'pick me up,' no?"

Later, in a nearby bar, he asked me if this was the first time I had cruised a member of an orchestra.

"On stage, and during Mahler's Ninth – yes," I replied.

"It has never happened to me before, but it was a very interesting experience to find such an attractive man's eyes fixed on me. I think that I played much better," he said, "and more passionately."

His comment disarmed me, not because of its thinly concealed expectations, but for the unusual reaction it created in me. To my surprise, I could not engage myself with him in any way. I found that I was now completely unrelated to this person who sat before me. I felt emptied, disinterested, and detached, and the last thing that I could have done was to share my fantasy with him. I knew instinctively that he wanted me, but I had taken him, and he was already becoming just another memory.

I moved the conversation back to the growth of Berlin, by which time I had finished my beer.

"You played with so much emotion this evening," I said, as I rose to leave, feeling that I should at least show him a minimum of generosity. "You gave me more pleasure than you can know – thank you."

He looked surprised, but made no attempt to delay me. At the door I looked back and his gaze was still on me – now puzzled.

Outside, the rain had stopped, and a milder wind had shaped dry patches in the pavement's wetness. The sounds of the city began to wrap around me as I walked quickly towards the U-Bahn.

The Moment

MAYA DAVIS

I SLEPT DEEPLY after a tiring train journey from Souillac. In a small pension with a bidet near the bed, and a toilet and clawfoot tub down the hall. Crisp, rose-scented sheets and a wide-silled window that opened to pigeons cooing under the eaves.

I check out in the early afternoon and trundle my two small duffels and battered leather satchel off to Gare du Nord. The Eurostar to London is delayed for three hours so I stow everything but the satchel in a locker.

As I stroll along the nearby streets I practice the art of going nowhere, doing nothing. Eventually I find myself outside Montparnasse Cemetery where curiosity brings this meditative game to an end.

The vastness of the cemetery, with its verdant lushness, sur-prises me as I walk through the large black gates. A paved walkway leads to a distant roundabout with benches and a single tall tree. The architectural line, and the way it draws my eye, is reminiscent of formal English garden design.

I meander through the grounds, stopping to read inscriptions on some of the more ornate graves and mausoleums. My favourites are the free-standing walled shrines with their locked iron-gated entrances. Like mini churches, protecting the enclosed relics of a life: bits of cloth, ornately-framed photos, china cups, even silver candlesticks. In one, several thin plaits of auburn hair are visible through the wrought-iron gate. A poignant and sentimental remem-brance.

Walking on, I come upon a stone crypt thickly covered in moss. The slate marker is adorned with a garland of vines and flowery script. LILIANNE MARIE ROUSSEL 1894 – 1910. Only sixteen years old. I imagine her to be a wan figure, languishing amidst the green-ery of a country garden, her frail face dominated by the flushed cheeks of a consumptive.

I hope her spirit won't mind me resting for a few moments against the rise of her grave, for it is situated under the shade of an enormous oak tree and the afternoon sun is oppressive. Lying back against the stone, I watch an old woman tidy a nearby grave, refreshing faded flowers with new blossoms.

To my left, about 100 metres away, a burial is in progress. The black clad mourners cross themselves repeatedly. Funerals in France are a serious business, but as with all things French, these solemn proceedings are undertaken with a certain élan that takes precedence over the formality.

There don't appear to be any other people about, except for a man with Mediterranean features making charcoal rubbings of elab-orate grave markers. Perhaps he is a history student or an artist.

I listen to the birds and other sounds of life in this place of final slumber. The breeze carries the low murmur of the priest's voice as he conducts the nearby graveside service.

Opening my eyes periodically to follow the dark-haired man's progress, I watch discreetly as his work brings him closer to my rest-ing place. He is tall and solid, masculine in a well-bred way.

Lulled by the heat, I drift into daydreams and startle when his warm, deep voice addresses me. "*Scusi, signorina,*" he says, gestur-ing to Liliane's gravestone. He's Italian, not French.

Nodding a greeting to him, I begin to rise to my feet so he'll have room to cover the swirling stone vines with stiff crackling parch-ment. But he motions for me to remain as I am. Sitting back down, I turn my head to watch him work at his task. Long-fingered hands move the nub of charcoal. Black covers white. The rhythmic rasping of charcoal over paper mesmerizes.

Hands clasped around my knees, I pretend to watch the rubbing process, but stare at him instead. Commit to memory the day's growth of beard, his olive skin, and blue-black hair. Admire his immaculately cut linen trousers, burgundy leather belt, and mus-cled arms left bare by a sleeveless cotton shirt. I feel my face slack-en slightly with unbidden desire.

He must see the look on my face. Or perhaps he instinctually senses the reaction of my body, for he responds with a look of inti-macy.

The rubbing is finished. Still reclining against the gravesite, I look up to say "Ciao," but the sight of an erection straining under his trousers draws my pupils downward. Finally looking into his face, our eye contact sets off a shared and primal chemical reaction. We are bathed in sunlight and the kind of instant attraction that can happen between people.

My body thrums with a silent need to be known by this man, a need so deep it's beyond physical. This is one of those rare moments in life that transcend rational explanation. When, from the briefest of connections between strangers there arises a sense of familiarity. Like fingers telling the beads of an ancient rosary or the murmurs of prayers so ingrained one mustn't actually think the words or they can't be spoken.

When he extends his hand to help me up, I take it because it's been so long since I felt this connection of spirit.

His hand is smooth but for a jagged area on his thumb. Warm and rough. He leads me to a mid-nineteenth-century mausoleum. Four greying brick walls, a moss-covered stone roof, and an ornate gate for an entrance. He unlocks the gate with a tarnished silver key that turns quietly.

Still holding my hand, he leads me within, then takes my satchel from me and stows it on the earthen floor along with his papers and charcoal sticks.

In a shrine to the dead, I am kissing this stranger who isn't a stranger. The scent of dust and dampness and ancient rose petals permeates my senses. My rational mind wonders if this is really happening, but my less cognitive soul accepts.

Cold marble welcomes the flushed skin on either side of my spine through my thin summer chemise as I lean against the wall for support. Eyes closed, I give up intentional thought. The smell of his sweat intoxicates, and his powerful muscles dominate. His hard penis presses against my soft belly through the fabric of our clothes, unafraid of disclosure. There is no self-awareness or pride, we are just here together, present in the moment.

Taking his hand and bringing it under my dress, I use the long fingers to caress my bare legs with the slow gentle circles of lovers comfortable together. We don't speak. Instead he suckles the swell of my upper lip and I trace the outline of his lower lip with my tongue.

His rough thumb scrapes my skin. When he tries to avoid

touching me with it, my fingers hold him close so the callus moves again and again over my pores.

Then it is my fingers that are enclosed. Without disturbing the rhythm of this moment, he takes hold of my right hand and together we slide through the wet warmth between my thighs. Rubbing and stroking so tenderly I begin to cry. I remember something I never knew, a memory of a time where everything that should be, was. Where there was no threshold and no conclusion.

I touch my cheek to his, salty tears catching in the comforting stubble of beard. My body aches in expectation of impending release. The muscles of my pelvis pulse in synchronicity with my heart, like second hands ticking round a clock face to the chime of my climax.

I give myself wholly to an orgasm that is brutal in its intensity. Spiritually I'm held in this precious moment. Physically, I am held on my feet by the strength of his body. I inhale the scent of man and soil and old stone.

Our arms wrap around each other. Silent and still but for the vibration of my heart against our joined chests and the throb of his still sheathed penis against my groin.

I sink to my knees before him. I unbuckle his belt. The sound of his zipper echoes against the marble walls. Expensive trousers and boxers fall to his ankles. Peeling back his foreskin, I take him into my mouth, stroking the soft exposed skin with my tongue. Looking up, we hold each other's glance as his penis rubs against the inside of my cheek.

"Bella, bella," he whispers. "Bella, bella, bella." A hymn, a chant, an adoration. We relax together, moving in unison like strangers who aren't.

When his hand tightens in my hair, I close my eyes and receive. Now it is he who weeps.

There are no words between us. I turn my head to the side and press it against his taut thighs. My kneecaps soften into the earthen floor; the downy hair on his legs so soft against my cheek. His hands stroke my hair with gentle passion. We rest like this.

Then, at the same time we reach out to clasp hands and he helps me to my feet. Together we silently gather our belongings and step through the open iron gate into the warmth of the afternoon sun. He shuts the gate behind us, turns the key in the lock, and reaches to hold my face between his hands.

Soft lips connect two lives, eternally sealing the impermanence of our encounter. We walk away from each other. Not looking back, not speaking, not manipulating the moment. Just being.

The Pink City, India

JEAN SMITH

HEAT SEDATES. Sway with the train, loose, a bareback rider. Rose dust collects in new hollows above pronounced clavicles. Rub dust between fingers, silky, wipe fingers across shirt front, ribs like letter-openers in leather sheaths. Slide under the elastic waistband of loose pants, touch hip bones, protruding like horns coming in on a young goat. Bony all over. Gulp thick mango syrup from a family-size bottle of squash – sickeningly sweet. It's supposed to be mixed with water. People watch. I am exotic. Foolish.

The desert air is brilliantly clear. The train speaks in forgettable repetition. Once it changes its tune, it's hard to remember what it used to say. For now it's chanting, "Don't go out with men I feel sorry for." The rhythm of the train turns into the clattering of a movie projector, metal reels wobble and squeak. Segments of sharp light flash through the windows, individual frames in slow motion. The soundtrack repeats, "These men will feel sorry for you for being with them." The heat renders me submissive to my imagination. A village in the Alps, a deep cold lake, an ornately gilded theatre, in the dark, sprawled across the projectionist's lap, I push my tongue into Swiss cheese holes as smooth and moist as skin.

On the other side of the muttering train, smooth rocks immobilized, half-sunk in the cracked earth where a river used to be, in another season the train will chatter off-key, "I'm happy again, I've forgotten. I'm happy again." Centuries of scraping the earth from the cliff beside me has left a spectrum of pinks: powder-puff, Pepto-Bismol, strawberry ice cream. "Jaipur is known as The Pink City. The temples, palaces, houses, and shops were constructed with the pink earth," the guidebook says. "In more recent times it has become law – all buildings must be pink. Pink paint is used on newer structures." And there it is, candy pink nuggets, embedded in the barren desert.

Metal against metal. The train stops. The city is still several miles away. "It's probably something on the tracks," says the elegantly dressed man standing in the aisle. Traditional long shirt and matching loose pants, but the fabric is raw silk dyed an iridescent burnt orange. Wavy black hair longer than most Indian guys. "Excuse me," he says, leaning over me, trying to see up the side of the train. I'm all the way back in my seat, his shirt draping across my face. Leaning farther, his shirt falls open. I'm inches from his flat brown stomach. Scent of coconut oil and warm skin.

Pushing back from the window, he says, "You should be in first class."

"I have a second class ticket."

"Then at least you should be in the women's compartment."

He motions with his head to the front of the train. I pull out my duffle bag, walk up the aisle and slide open the door of the women's compartment. Six women holding bowls of food-stained rice are wedged in with baskets and bundles. I close the door and walk back. Iridescent orange has taken my seat.

"We've run over a cow. It happens quite a lot on this section of track. You're going to Jaipur?"

"Yes."

"Are you travelling alone? Where are you staying?"

"How long does it take to get a cow out?" I ask.

"They're saying it is quite jammed in. Maybe half an hour. You should be careful in the city, especially near the train station. Taxi drivers will try to take you all over the place and then to the hotels on the other side of town."

"The same as all the cities," I say, asserting myself as a veteran traveler.

"It seems a little bit worse here for some reason."

He sounds sincere. Smiling, looking straight into my eyes, my unusual blue eyes. Sunlight illuminates particles of pink dust in the air, swirling between us, glinting off and on. Can he see their planes igniting, twinkling like stars? Shimmer turns into sizzle staring into translucent amber eyes. Dry throat, swallow and lick lips, sweet mango. Ears plugged up, ocean waves roar, empty moonshell, thudding skull. Dense tidal waves pull through me, directed by gravity, light and heat, mangos, coconuts and warm skin, uninhabited seashells and waves. Shift of breeze, the dust changes direction. Jumping up gracefully, he offers me my seat.

"When we get there I'll help you find a reliable driver. I know a good hotel quite close to the station." Voice is ballast, counterbalance, an even keel.

"No, thank you, I can find my own hotel."

"Suit yourself." He reaches into his leather satchel. "Let me give you my card. If you have any problems, please give me a call."

I take the card and dismiss the name as unpronounceable. Below it: Jeweller, a Jaipur address, and a New York address. Seventh Avenue. I start to hand it back. He laughs. "Keep it. Call me. I'd be happy to show you around." The train moves backwards, pauses, and starts toward the city.

"And you would be who?" he asks in a space between train whistles.

Names of planets pop into my head. Planet, from the Greek, wanderer. Saturn? Pluto?

"Venus," I answer, affording myself the luxury of lying to a man I will never see again.

———

The train station is a nightmare. Beggars, cripples, orphans, taxi drivers, and tour guides swarm around me; I can't get to the street. Someone grabs my elbow, I pull away. It's the jeweller, still smiling. I relax a little. "I see what you mean. I didn't expect it to be worse than Delhi."

"We don't see so many tourists here in Jaipur. It seems your arrival is a bit of a special occasion." He reaches for my bag. "Here, let me help you."

"I can carry it."

"I'm sure you can, but allow me."

We move through the crowd without any problem. He tosses my bag in the trunk of a taxi and we're off into the chaos of trucks, bikes, rickshaws, cows, and camels clogging the Pink City's streets. Two blocks away the driver skids to a stop; laughing and coughing we step out into a cloud of pink dust. The jeweller swings my bag over his shoulder and points towards a pedestrian tunnel. In the dark he stops, puts his hand on the back of my neck, and pulls me to him, his lips brushing against my cheek. He clamps onto my earring, rolling it around in his mouth, flicking it with his tongue, biting loudly. I shudder. Teeth against metal. I grab his shoulders to stay close to him, ready to push him away as soon as he lets go. He moves from my earring to my neck, kissing a trail across my shoulder. I pull away and walk on. We step into a courtyard. He greets the hotel owner, and announces my need for a room. Turning back to me, he bows, "I'll be back in two hours. We'll visit the tailor, you'll be fitted for a new outfit, then I will take you to dinner. A really good dinner."

My lips part, ready to refuse.

"Don't worry so much," he says, leaning forward. He kisses his fingertip and taps it on my nose. "I'll see you in a little while."

The owner throws open a door and motions me into a rebelliously deep blue room. I close the door without turning on the light, and sit on the edge of the sagging bed while my eyes adjust to the dark. I'm disappointed in myself. I should have told him not to come back. But I haven't had dinner with anyone, I've barely spoken to anyone, in over a month. Flopping backwards on the bed, springs jab me in the ribs.

———

Knocking wakes me. The room is dark. I find the door and open it.

"Oh-oh. You were asleep."

"Give me a minute," I say, closing the door to blackness. I feel around in space for a light-chain, arms swimming. Nothing. I open the door again.

"No light. I'll leave the door open." I splash water on my face at the sink, the mirror is nailed six inches too high on the wall. He is watching me, arms folded, leaning in the doorway, enjoying my lack of privacy. I jump up to see a split second of reflection, fingers through hair, I walk towards him, stopping in front of his silhouette. I can't see his expression. He reaches out for me, I take his hands and push him away. Twisting loose he grabs my wrists, takes a step into the room, and closes the door with his foot. He holds me close. Frozen in blackness, up swirls away from down, aviation instruments fail just prior to smashing into the surface of the sea, passion splattering into the depths. Rustling hair against my ear, radio frequencies tuning across the dial, searching for a station, a point on a line. I want to be free of adding moments up into something else, to accept everything as it is, spliced together out of sequence. Stalled here in darkness, his body blinding me with closeness, pressure gathering in the metre of my heart, the intensity of passion is taking over. My hips push against him. He breathes roughly and releases me and it is he who reaches for the door.

The daylight is disorienting. My desire is stronger since his rejection. Preoccupation with fending him off has shifted; I want to get him alone.

I pull the door closed behind me.

"No key?" I ask, bending down to look at the doorknob.

"No lock," he points at the owner, asleep in a chair. "He'll keep an eye on it."

"Right," I say, trying to remember this man's name.

———

The old tailor holds up a bolt of dark blue silk.

"To match your eyes," the jeweller says, unreeling a length of fabric. He binds it tightly around me, runs his hands down my back, around my waist, and up to my breasts, spreading his fingers and squeezing.

My lips tremble. The tailor approaches with his measuring tape; the jeweller snaps it from him and wraps it around my chest, he calls out a number. He measures my waist, then drops to his knees to adjust the twisted tape around my hips. When the tailor turns away to consider his calculations, the jeweller puts his face between my legs and lightly sinks his teeth in. I moan and grab the back of his head to hold his mouth near my clenching cunt. I can feel his rapid breath, moist, through the light fabric. I spread my legs and I rub his face on my throbbing pussy. The jeweller jumps to his feet, dusts off his knees, smiling, always smiling. I am dizzy and perhaps a little pale. I lean against a stack of fabric and unravel myself from the silk, noticing the wet spot where his mouth had been.

"Are you all right?" he asks.

"No, not exactly."

"Let's go and sit down somewhere. I would like to have a conversation with you, Venus," he says awkwardly.

Venus, Venus. How did I come up with that? The planets, the wanderer, the illuminated dust seem like years ago. What did his business card say? I'm ready to fuck this guy and I don't know his name. And he thinks I'm Venus. I laugh. He laughs, too.

———

After a tour of the city and a spicy-sweet tea, we return to pick up my new clothes. The tailor flings them across the counter with a proud flourish. The fabric is different, it is shiny black satin, not the blue to match my eyes. The tailor points at a tapestry curtain.

"Well, put them on and let's go to dinner," says the jeweller, ignoring the obvious error.

Behind the curtain there are huge potted palms swaying, trapped in an oscillating wind from an electric fan. The fronds clatter against the wall energetically and then go limp. Incense wafts from a wall-sconce in trailing loops, like sky-writing, broken into words by the breeze. Beneath the canopy of shiny green palms a chaise lounge is piled with tasseled pillows. I sit down, unlace my boots and wiggle my toes on the cool tile floor. I exchange my clothes for the smooth black outfit – it's way too big. The jeweller pulls aside the curtain, steps forward, and lets it drop behind him.

"What's with all the buttons?" I ask, holding up the front of the shirt. He slides his hands under the satin, turns me around, and grinds his hard cock into the crack of my silky ass. The trouser legs are way too long; I bend over to roll them up and his cock slides farther between my legs, right where I want it. "It's too big," I say. He laughs and tightens his grip. "It will fit just fine, you'll see."

"I mean the clothes." He pulls the drawstring around my waist and the trousers fall into a shiny heap around my ankles. With both hands he grabs the shirt and rips it off, buttons tinkle across the tile floor, black tendrils of silk are suspended in the air. I gasp, he puts his hand softly over my mouth. The tailor yells, the jeweller yells back and makes a shushing sound at me. He takes his hand off my mouth. I lick my lips and kiss his "O"-shaped open mouth. He moves me backwards by the shoulders to the chaise lounge; he swipes off the pillows and guides me down. Sucking in his stomach, he puts his hand down his pants and grabs his cock. I pull his drawstring and twist out of my panties. His cock is between my legs immediately. I run my hands over his shoulders and down his back to his hips. I pull him towards me. Penetrating me gently he moans, he pushes farther. Wiggling beneath him I'm impatient for more. When he is completely inside he pauses, relaxing slightly in the ultimate closeness, completely connected. He slides out and re-enters more forcefully. I wrap my legs around him, arching my back. Pumping me desperately, his face is a contortion of desire and exertion. I tense up, on the verge of orgasm, he fucks steadily until my muscles grab and squeeze his cock. Deep inside, at the end of his final thrust, I feel his pulsating release. He lies down shakily and rests his head on my shoulder. Breathing punctuated by his pounding heart, he laughs and whispers, "Now what are you going to wear to dinner?"

"How about the blue-to-match-my-eyes outfit? It should be ready by now, don't you think?"

The Shirt

ROBIN METCALFE

THE STREET WHERE Randall Zinck has his store is bracketed between
busy thoroughfares. A torrent of traffic rushes past on either side of
the little neighbourhood. Occasionally a stray car wanders down the
street as if lost. In the park across from Randall's store, sunlight set-
tles through the trees like silt in a deep, slow pool. You can just hear
the sound of traffic above the rustling of the leaves.

The faded letters on the tall, old-fashioned windows of Randall's
store say ZINCK'S ARMY SURPLUS, but one can find all sorts of old
clothes, not to mention camping supplies, among the dusty racks.
Randall is both the proprietor and the only sales clerk. A tall, thin
man on the elderly side of middle age, Randall has the air of a deal-
er in rare and erotic antiquities, a connoisseur of the most exquisite
taste. His smile, while perfectly proper, is also somehow suggestive,
as if it harbours an indecent secret. I know what you are looking for,
it says, and I am quite certain you will find it here.

It is Randall's preference to deal in used clothing. For all their
flashy stylishness, new clothes are cheap and shallow things. They
have no history. Used clothing, even the most drab and tattered, is
steeped in the past, in that most mysterious kind of history, the personal, the unknown. For what is unknown must be imagined, and
how much vaster and more complex is the geography of the imagination compared with the plain streets of daily reality.

The first time I visited Randall's store, I found the jacket of my
dreams. An old high school jacket, probably of the fifties or late for-
ties, judging by the quality of the sturdy, navy wool cloth. The white
satin lining under the collar was yellowed but still intact, the pockets bordered with white leather piping. And on the shoulder – what
joy! – the name Steve, embroidered in silver thread. Who is Steve,

what is he? By now, he is probably married, middle-aged, dead. I don't want to know. I can see him bundled in blue wool during some ancient, innocent winter, going to basketball practice, walking his best friend home along the railway tracks, jerking off in his bedroom surrounded by pennants and Hardy Boys novels. I am in love with him. Every time I put on his jacket I become him, I put on his youth and his unknowing beauty. Strangers, misled by my small deception, address me by his name. Sometimes I correct them, sometimes I do not.

Randall always calls me Steve. He knows my real name, having seen it on my credit card when I made my first purchase. Nevertheless, he calls me Steve, out of respect for my fantasy. It has become our private joke. Since that first visit, he has treated me with a polite familiarity, as if he recognizes in me a kindred spirit. He smiles as the bell tinkles above the wooden door to announce my arrival and leads me to the bin of army-surplus footwear, where a pair of white canvas sneakers is waiting for me. A label sewn neatly to the underside of the tongue says that GAUTHIER, P.L., pulled these onto his sweaty feet more times than he would care to remember. I am enchanted, of course, and wear them home.

Three blocks from Randall's store, across from the army base on Gottingen Street, I crouch on the sidewalk to retie my shoelaces. A young man walks slowly past me, pauses, stops. I look up into the blue eyes of a pretty soldier with curly blond hair. He asks if I am from Windsor Park. Not understanding his question, I grunt noncommittally. He takes this to mean yes and suddenly smiles at me as if I were a long-lost brother. I am from his regiment, it seems – he recognizes the sneakers. Can he walk with me? (Can he!) Used clothing can be one of the most powerful aphrodisiacs.

———

It is a fine bright day in early summer. Too fine – I know I won't get any work done today. A good day to visit Randall's store.

The air is warm enough to get away with wearing only a t-shirt. Light green, armed-forces issue, with darker green trim at the neck and sleeves. A gift from the pretty blond soldier, who left in the halflight of early morning wearing one of mine. I can smell the odour of his golden skin trapped in the soft fabric. My armpits sprout dark hairs from under the sleeves where his blond hair would have glistened before. And after he left my bed – embarrassment of riches! – I found his jockey shorts, lost between the tangled sheets. The horny god of love smiles on me. I have them on now, beneath my blue jeans. The white cotton that cradled his hard little nuts is wrapped snugly around my balls. They roll inside their hairy sac as the juices stir within. My cock nuzzles against warm cloth.

Randall's street is nearly deserted in the lazy afternoon sun. Two old men doze on a park bench in the little square. The shop is hazy with dust as I open the front door. A tinny aria from *Tosca* drifts up from the portable cassette player propped against the cash register. Randall is bent over a newspaper that is spread out in front of him on the countertop. He looks up to greet me with a genteel nod and returns to his reading. The smoke from his cigarette plays hide-and-seek with the shafts of light that filter through the dirty windows. The air in the store is warm and stale.

Randall always lets me take my time poking through the tumbled bins of clothing. I linger over piles of combat boots, sneakers, t-shirts, dark-green army sweaters peppered with moth holes, military caps with the insignia removed. I try one of these on, but as usual it is far too small. Do soldiers all have tiny heads? Nothing here catches my interest. I move to the other side of the store, passing over the boxes of manufacturer's rejects and secondhand jackets. The table of used shirts is a circus of colours. I sort absently among garish paisleys and stripes, sniffing for the special find that makes the search worthwhile.

My fingers catch at a patch of dark cloth. I pull out a knit shirt with short sleeves. It is burgundy with fine yellow horizontal stripes. Nothing beautiful, but something about it holds my interest. Stretched and rumpled, it long ago lost its shape – or, rather, it gained a shape, that of the body it once clothed. The ghosts of biceps bulge at the sleeves, swelling pectorals stretch the chest, an invisible neck surges from the open collar. A faint male odour lingers about the fabric. Some unknown man has left his imprint here for me to snuggle into, as in the morning one might curl into the warm hollow left by a body that has gone on its way.

Ah, I see that one has found you. Randall regards me from behind his counter with that secret smile of his. That shirt is very special. You must try it on. He pauses to extinguish his cigarette with a delicate tap, then walks around the back of the counter and out into the store. Come. I'll open up the dressing room.

I follow Randall down the twisting aisles to the back of the store.

The path to the dressing room leads through a rack of World War II greatcoats, looming shaggy and black like old bison. We push through the herd of coats and out into a small back storage room, crowded with dusty boxes. To the left is a familiar cubicle with a curtain stretched across the opening. I move towards it. No, says Randall, not that one. Over here.

Randall turns a key in a lock and pushes open the door to a small room that I have not seen before. He flips on the light and it glares off white walls and ceiling. Here we are, says Randall. Take as long as you like. I step into the room and pull the door shut behind me.

The bareness of the room is a relief after the musty clutter of the store. It is larger than an ordinary dressing room. A chair upholstered in blue vinyl is positioned against the wall to my left. Across from it stretches a large mirror. And beneath the mirror, a clean white shelf with a glass bottle, a neatly folded towel, and a book.

I strip off my t-shirt and pause to admire myself in the mirror. I run my fingers lightly over the ripples on my stomach, bought with the agony of many thousands of sit-ups. The burgundy shirt is soft to the touch and tickles my nose as I pull it over my head. It flows like a cool hand across my skin. What man has worn this shirt before? I feel as if I am in contact with him now, through my contact with the shirt. I regard myself in the mirror. I have deliberately let the shirt fall carelessly. The collar is crumpled and crooked, the tail hangs out rumpled over my jeans. My hair is mussed up. I look like a tough. For a moment, I experience that delicious sensation of seeing myself as a stranger, someone glimpsed briefly on the street, perhaps a labourer. It's an ugly shirt and shows its age, the sort of shirt a man would wear to perform heavy physical work. To hoist garbage into a truck, perhaps. I smile at myself, a come-on to the stranger in the mirror. I strike a couple of poses.

My movements bring my eye back to the articles arranged on the shelf. They have been placed there as neatly and carefully as if on an altar. They are Randall's, I tell myself, and private, but my curiosity gets the better of me. I unscrew the cap of the bottle and take a cautious sniff. Ordinary vegetable oil. In a dressing room? I move on. The towel is antiseptically clean with a chemical odour, its virginity restored by detergent and bleach. If it has any secrets, it will not give them up. At last my hand hovers over the book. It is large with a black cover, a looseleaf binder I now realize, not an ordinary book. Carefully, as if trespassing, I turn back the cover.

The image startles me. For a moment I think I am looking again in the mirror. A dark-haired, muscular man gazes at me, his build as stocky as my own. He is wearing the same burgundy-and-yellow knit shirt that I am wearing now. But he is not me, of course. The man in the Polaroid photograph has a ragged moustache; I am clean-shaven. His hair is a cluster of playful curls, like that of a Greek faun. Mine is straight. Nevertheless, the resemblance is striking.

The next page holds another surprise. The same man, only now his hand has moved up from his side and reaches in towards the centre to grasp his cock, which is hard and exposed. The cloth of his jeans is peeled back in a wide V, his balls dangle free like pale fruit, the pink shaft points up towards his navel. More images follow, showing him pushing the shirt up over his chest, squeezing his balls, closing his eyes – and finally, in the last photograph, trailing his fingers through a shiny puddle of white smeared across his belly. I gaze at this last image with rapt attention, my hand pressed against the growing bulge in my jeans, gently kneading the eager flesh.

Did I say the last photograph? I meant the last of him. For the next page begins a new series, this time of a slender young blond man with long, lank hair. The burgundy shirt hangs loosely over his flat belly. This one has his pants off entirely, posing with his cock in his hand, smirking at the camera. His eyes remain wide open right through to the final photograph, watching the white liquid come threading out into the air. My own cock is pounding at the tight fabric of my jeans.

The photographs continue. I plunge into them as if deeper into a dream. There must be at least a dozen men. I start to count, but keep losing my concentration. A thin man with close-cut brown hair, as stern and serious as a schoolteacher, his cock a ruler pointing upward. A middle-aged man, grizzled and masculine, thick hair sprouting from his powerful arms and from the open neck of the burgundy shirt. A soldier with a tiny black moustache and a tattoo on the bulge of his upper arm, gazing from the photograph with deep, liquid eyes. His cock aims straight out of the picture like a gun. A dozen men, standing before a white wall, their cocks hard for the camera, jerking off one by one. Eyes open or closed, cocks straight or curved, cut or uncut, all joined in the animal ritual of coming.

The mirror presents me, spotlit in a white room like an actor in the opening scene of a play. The script lies open before me. I examine the mirror more closely. The glass is dark, like the mirrors in police questioning rooms. Not all the light is being reflected. I press my face against the glass and peer into a silver void. I see my own eyes glistening in the shadow of my hand. My reflection steps back and smiles at me. We know what to do next.

I take my time starting, rubbing the hard ridge that has risen in my jeans. Deliberately, with a tantalizing slowness, I open the fly, gingerly lift out the tender balls, the long pink root of my cock. The edge of the shirt brushes against the tip of my cock, a maddening sensation that makes it stiffen and point upward. My hand strokes soothingly up and down. Horniness seems to flow into my groin from the shirt. The mirror turns me into my own porn star, one of a series. Tinker Tailor Soldier Sailor. Me, I'm the Garbage Man. Stick out yer can. I have ceased to be me and have become an ideal type: Man with Hard-on.

My balls are framed by the folded-back flaps of my jeans. The pressure on the underside of my cock is pleasant, but the pants are becoming an encumbrance. I peel them off and feel the sweet freedom of air tingling against my bare ass. My cock waves in the air like a flag. I prance about the room, horny as a goat, grabbing my stiff dick and eyeing myself in the mirror. My cock feels as if a dozen hard cocks were stuffed inside it, the dozen hard-ons of the men who have worn the shirt before me.

The mirror makes the room a closed circuit. There is nowhere to look except at my own reflection. My flickering glance cruises the stranger in the mirror. I am alone with my eyes, my cock and the burgundy shirt. I leer at myself lustfully, strutting and grinning like a bare-assed satyr. The joy of prancing begins to fade. I settle into the chair for some serious pleasure. As my sweaty behind makes its clammy contact with the cold vinyl, I remember again that I am bare-assed. The sticky surface squeaks the word as I wriggle about, whispers it to my cock, which is trembling with frustration, but I won't let it come, not yet.

Ever so slowly, I peel back the soft velvet blanket of my foreskin. The flesh beneath is swollen to a slick, glistening red. My dry fingers are raw against the tender skin. As I reach towards the shelf, I thank my thoughtful benefactor for the provision of the slippery golden oil the bottle contains.

I cannot put it off any longer. As the pressure mounts, I give in to the pounding rhythm of my fist, give myself over to the spirit of Horny Man that inhabits the shirt, that is possessing me as the hot tide rises within me. Even the image in the mirror is squeezed out of consciousness as my eyes close and I am lost to spurting, surging pleasure. In the moment of serene silence that follows, I hear only my own heartbeat and a faint mechanical click and whirr from somewhere behind the glass.

––––––––

Randall is sitting behind the counter when I come out again into the store. He smiles and raises his head from the paper before him. An interesting garment, is it not? I nod and smile in return. Too bad it is not for sale, he sighs – it is part of my personal collection; it would never do to break up the set.

The bell above the door tinkles over my head. The sound of *Tosca* trails after me, out into the sunlit street.

155

Let's Twist Again

LEO CULLEN

MAM GAVE ME TEN CIGARETTES to have at the dance. "Don't drink, but smoke," she said. "A person who neither drinks nor smokes is mean. Don't drink." She appraised me. "Close the middle button of your jacket," she said. I did. "No, that's not right. Close the lower button instead. Don't look so miserable. Smile. Ah, that's better. He looks like Frank Sinatra, doesn't he." Daddy laughed and said he didn't know what Frank Sinatra looked like. Mam sighed, as nice a sigh as I ever heard.

My big brother Richie was jingling the keys of the car all the time Mam was fixing me. "Hurry on," he said. I didn't know if he liked the look of me. He picked up Thos and Fern at the Cross. They looked okay, even if their suits were a bit old-fashioned. Then he picked up Vere Hunt who was standing by the piers at the end of his avenue and I got in the back, letting Vere in my seat. "Cashel or Thurles," said Vere, "or Las Vegas?" He thumped out a dance with his feet against the floor of the car and brushed a fleck off his light-blue suit. I didn't know him. "Hello," he said to me. "Another woman chaser." Did that mean I looked all right?

"Hands up for Cashel," said Richie. He was driving in that direction anyway, flying it.

Thos and Fern discussed Cashel.

"Still the best place," Thos said.

"For what?" laughed Fern. He poked Thos with his elbow. Vere Hunt laughed at them. "Two old goats," he said. With a flick of his fingers, he spun a cigarette butt out the open window. Good shot, I thought.

"Hands up for where, young Kennedy," he said to me.

"Cashel," I said.

"Hah, who has a date tonight?" Fern asked. Now they were laughing at me.

I did not have a date tonight. Next week was my date. A date next week with Frieda. I wasn't telling the others, though. I wouldn't tell them. I didn't like the word date. The word sounded wrong, inappropriate. Wrong for us, me and my one and only love, Frieda.

We watched the dancers from the balcony. That was how you learned. Watching fellows like Vere Hunt; he was the best jiver in the hall. Slow numbers were easy. You just sort of stuck to your partner and went into the middle of the dancers. Then you were moved round and round under the crystal ball. Jiving was not easy. I could have watched Vere Hunt jive all night. From watching Vere I knew one thing: I wasn't ready to take the floor yet.

I practiced a slow descent of the wide, shallow-stepped stairs. The carpet was plush beneath my feet. It felt good. If any girls happened to be looking up, they could appraise me. They mightn't yet have the pleasure of dancing with me, but at least they could get a foretaste of my Frank Sinatra-like movements. But Dickie Rock was singing, one hand over his heart and the other wavering before him as if he was divining water or something, and even in the dim light of the hall I could see all the faces looking up towards him, and every now and then, little whoops of admiration. Dickie grabbed his microphone and shook the flex like he was cracking a whip. A layer of dust the colour of face-compact rippled above the swaying crowd. Nobody was noticing Frank Sinatra on the stairs.

I went into the gents. There was nobody in there. It must have been because everybody, even the learners, had taken the floor for the slow number. I was able to look at myself in the mirror. Normally you couldn't get near the mirror because of the queue of fellows combing their hair before it. Fellows had to stoop or bend sideways or rise on tippy-toes to get a glimpse at themselves. There could be ten faces all crowded into the little mirror at the same time. Now there was only me. Maybe it was because I was receiving the mirror's undivided attention, but my face was all thin, and all the colour was withdrawn from it and the hair was weak as paper. No girl would ever even look at such a child's face. Then somebody came in and I had to look away and I went over to the urinals. The fellow was Vere Hunt. I knew the light blue suit. He stood at the urinal right beside mine. He was making a very loud splash against the urinal and I hoped he wasn't listening to me because I was barely managing to make any splash. He was smoking a cigarette. He took it out of his mouth as he kept on splashing. I was finishing now so I had to slow it down. It was that or leave, and be thought little of by Vere Hunt. Then he pulled out his comb. Both hands were in use now: one holding a cigarette, the other combing the hair and the splashing going on louder than ever. I didn't know how he was managing to hold his laddie-boy out without any hands. Nonchalance, I had to suppose, that was what was doing it. Then he put his comb away, put his cigarette back in his mouth and, with both hands, furiously shook himself. "Hardy night," he said to me. "And how's young Kennedy?" His shoes clicked on the tiles as he walked out, not waiting for my response. "Watch out ladies, Vere Hunt is coming to get you," he said. The smoke was getting into his eyes and deliciously blinding him. There was clapping going on, then Dickie Rock was on the microphone: "Thank you ladies and gentlemen, next dance. And take your partners please." Supposing Frieda had another boyfriend, supposing he was somebody like Vere Hunt – well then, I was sunk.

That was the first time I went dancing.

And now had come the second time: Donie Collins and his Showband. In silver suits. Donie sang.

I had gone for the practice the first time. It was too late this time for practice; this time was it. Life had suddenly moved me into a faster lane and I had to try and keep up with it. The recent correspondence. That's what brought about the change of pace. The sudden impulse to write to Frieda, after all those years since primary school days together. The bulging twelve-page letter, written on both sides and smuggled into her boarding-school. I got one page back in return:

> *Thank you for your letter. Everybody in our dormitory says you have lovely handwriting. Re. your marriage proposal. Should the bride wear white? Ha ha. I will be going dancing every Sunday during the Summer, viz, Cashel Ballroom.*
>
> *NB: I have to make the best of this Summer because next Summer I am becoming a nun. Joke.*
>
> *PS: Can you drive?*
>
> *I remain your sugarlumps, Frieda.*
>
> *PPS: Not the first Sunday in the hols. The second one.*

Frieda's letter depressed me. I hated the tone. All this grown-up style of viz's, NB's, and jokes. She sounded far too sophisticated for me. And so casual: "Not the first Sunday." Well, where was she going to be on the first Sunday then?

But, here we were on the second Sunday: "One for the money, two for the show, three get ready and go go go." Donie Collins was sweating.

The girls were lined up along one side of the floor and the men, as they pushed past, were reviewing them. I got myself into the middle of the crush of men. With my heart jumping, I began looking for Frieda.

We were dancing very slowly, in short steps. "You can dance every dance with the guy that gives you the eye, let him hold you tight...." She smelled different. Not like in the old days in the lanes: fresh-airy and cowslippy she smelled then. Now she smelled like a woman. It took a while getting used to. And lipstick, and mascara.... The brown dress clung to her. And the hand over my shoulder was holding a box of cigarettes. Oh, Frieda, Frieda, I wanted to say, you are the same to me as ever. Your two front teeth that once long ago you chipped when you had a fall are still as chipped, as lovely. The openness they bestowed upon your face was what first arrested me and still it does. You have no idea how much I love you. It is not fair how much I love you. But did I say all that?

No. I was too intent on keeping in step. A one two, a one two three.... And on keeping a distance of at least arms' length between us. And on not staring directly at her. Because some things about her were different. Her hair, unrecognizable from the days when it had been straight and unkempt, was arranged in ringlets that fell forward and bobbed upon her breasts. Had I been drawn to that part of her before? She was like a pony. I was paralyzed with the strange new beauty of her.

I had three dances with Frieda. What did that mean? What was I supposed to do now? She was looking up at me with a sort of openness, or of trust, that suggested her compliance in whatever I decided to do. That worried me a little. She didn't seem at all the same person who had written me the flippant note. Once, when Vere Hunt was dancing nearby, he winked at her and, though more modest about it, she winked back. But my confidence was growing. There had been a fast dance: Donie, doing Chubby Checker, putting on that lovely dusty distant desire of Chubby's voice. "Let's twist again like we did last summer, let's twist again, like we did last year...." I had found myself surprisingly adept. In an unstructured way I could move around to the beat. I still could not jive like Vere Hunt. Vere kept his dancing tight and controlled, he and his partner always surrounded by a circle of empty floor. Like a spotlight was on him; making him, in his blue suit and coiffed hair, the main attraction on the floor. However, in a fashion that was loose and easy, I could master the Twist. I could move. That was why, when Richie walked over to me and whispered instructions, I did not panic.

"Shift her now before the dance is over."

"Okay."

"Here's the keys to the car."

"No, I don't want them." I didn't want the car, everybody looking in the window at me and Frieda. Privacy, I wanted. Privacy, I judged, was the essential ingredient of love.

"Okay with me," Richie said. "If you don't want them I'll use the car myself, you take her for a walk."

I took Frieda for a very long walk. Privacy was hard to come by in Cashel that night. There were couples in every doorway, in every lane. Undignified sights, I thought. Sometimes huddled darkly, sometimes smirking out at me, cigarettes glowing in the night like cats' eyes. Were we to be as undignified as that? No thanks. I kept walking us at a steady trot up the hill to the Rock of Cashel, the music from the dancehall following behind us. Where better place, I was thinking to myself, than the Rock for privacy: Long ago castle of Ireland's High Kings and Bishops – nowadays the quietest spot you could find. Frieda wore a bright yellow coat with shaggy nylon tufts and every time we walked beneath a street light it shone. It was a startling coat, but it was lovely. We looked lovely together, I thought. She in her coat, me in my suit.

"How far have we to walk?"

"Just a little farther."

"It's an awful climb." She was running out of breath. "Can we stop?"

"Just a little farther." I still felt the prying eyes.

We had to climb a high wall with stone steps built into it.

"What are you taking me in there for?" she asked from the top of the wall.

"I want to show you something."

"What?"

"King Cormac's chapel."

"Oh, Jesus."

But she came. There were no steps down the other side of the wall. "Can you get down?" I asked. "Can you help me?" she answered. I had to hold her legs, guide her feet into crevices of the wall. My hands nearly fell off me with the feel of her nylons. I had to look up as she descended. "Put your foot there, now there." Up her coat I saw, it couldn't be helped: her white knickers, beautiful as they sailed past me, beautiful as the moon sailing through the clouds. Then we were both on the ground and I was holding her hand and a thought was going through my mind that we would not be able to climb out. It was a high climb without any steps. We would be on the Rock for the night. I wondered if she would mind. I wouldn't. She clattered across the stones with me in her high heels, spirited as a foal. Maybe it was getting her away from the dancehall and the lights that had done it. We were not meant for restrictive places like that, the high outdoors was for us. Higher and higher we climbed, flitting beneath archways, the yellow coat illuminated, then cast in shadow.

King Cormac's chapel was locked. "Up here," she said. She was my old Frieda now. As in those adventurous days when we were childhood sweethearts. She led me along a wall which dropped on one side so that with a flip of your stomach you could only barely look on the slope of the Rock below. We went into a sort of room. We could look out over the country and the town.

And there we kissed and I felt the fur of her coat against my face. Me, in the Rock of Cashel, and I feeling the safest I had ever felt in my life.

I loved the kissing. I found it the most silent and sweetest of occupations. How I wished it could have gone on forever. But of course nothing is forever. For I'd had suddenly to get into a talking mood. I'd had to. A problem had arisen: the laddie-boy, it was misbehaving. Stumbling forward on a journey of its own. An embarrassing situation. Something I'd never before had to cope with. I tried to distract her attention from me: "Thank you for coming up here," I was going on. "Here is where Saint Patrick converted the High King. Patrick's staff pierced into his foot and he thought it was part of the ceremony, imagine that!"

"The poor eejit," Frieda said. I was talking on and on. Meanwhile, my body and mind were going in different directions. While my kisses were telling their own sweet story, I was having at the same time to stand edgeways to Frieda. I bulwarked my hip against her, my front faced away and out towards the drop at the window. My kisses were sweet; I could not let her know about the not so sweet state of the rest of me. I knew it looked stupid. I felt like I was the gable end of a house or something. But what could I do?

"Your hip, it's hurting me."

"Sorry."

I did a partial pirouette towards her, but not completely. We kissed.

"Sorry, is my hip still hurting you?"

"Yes."

"Sorry."

"What was it you said you wanted to show me, anyway?"

It wasn't what I wanted to show her, but I did.

We lay down, whose idea I didn't know. "Twelve o'clock Rock." I could hear the song from below, clear as day, coming up the hill and over the wall. Donie Collins: "A one two three o'clock, four o'clock rock." All the lights of Cashel were down there. You could see them reflected in the sky. All the Plain of Tipperary lying around the Rock of Cashel in semi-light. And beyond, heading for Devil's Bit Mountain, the darkness. That was the last dance. A silence fell. Frieda's dress had a slit down the side. Why had I not noticed it during the dancing? She put my hand in. Then the National Anthem got going. "Laa la la la la," went the tenor-sax. And for Frieda, sweet Frieda, I rose stiffly to attention. Then it happened inside me. One light touch of Frieda's fingers. That did it. A touch up along the back of the stiff soldier and inside in me a tightening exploded. Like a tree, roots and all, shattered in a lightning storm. And then everything that for years had been trying to fall out of me was falling, first shooting off and then falling, windfalls onto mossy ground. Then I was crying, tears and wet everywhere, and Frieda was telling me it was all right.

"I love you more than the world," I said. "Do you know that?"

Frieda was telling me it was all right, pet.

Then she was wiping me with her fingers, down there where the shaking had subsided, putting her fingers in her mouth and licking the wet off.

"What are you doing?" I said.

"You're salty and nice."

I was having to look away. The storm had calmed, but not the tears tilting down my face. "No, you're nice."

"Pet," she was still saying. "It's all right."

I heard the doors of cars banging shut and engines starting down below. I was saying, it's not all right. We won't be able to climb out of here. We're stuck.

Frieda found a way out, a gap where the wall had collapsed at its base so that only the top part remained. She laughed going under the arch of it, uncrumpling her coat and dress. I followed, thinking of the taste of salt and feeling all the wind of Tipperary blow in my direction through the gap broken in the rocks and freeze me where I was still wet.

Authors

CARELLIN BROOKS has had sex in London, Paris, Tokyo, and New York. During her years abroad she favoured public toilets, moving cars, and parks. Unfortunately, she was unable to write about any of these encounters with much in the way of skill. Brooks edited *Bad Jobs: My Last Shift at Albert Wong's Pagoda and Other Ugly Tales of the Workplace* (Arsenal Pulp Press, 1998) and is co-editing *Carnal Nation: New Sex Fictions* (Arsenal Pulp Press, 2000).

NATALEE CAPLE is the author of two books of fiction: *The Heart is Its Own Reason* (Insomniac Press, 1998) and *The Plight of Happy People in an Ordinary World* (House of Anansi, 1999), and one book of poetry: *A More Tender Ocean* (Coach House Press, 2000). She is the Literary Editor of *The Queen Street Quarterly*. Her poetry and fiction have been published across Canada in *The Malahat Review*, *The Capilano Review*, *Descant*, *Canadian Literature*, *Grain*, *The New Quarterly*, and many other magazines. Her work is taught at the University of Ohio in the Creative Writing program. She lives in Toronto.

NELL CARBERRY is a writer living in Brooklyn. Her work has been published in *BUST*, *Bitch*, *Paramour*, and *Libido*. Her story "The Manicure," appears in *Best American Erotica 2000*, edited by Susie Bright.

M. CHRISTIAN has published over 100 short stories in a wide variety of venues. Some of his erotic stories can be found in *Best Gay Erotica 2000, Friction, Best American Erotica, The Mammoth Book of Short Erotic Novels, Quickies 2, Viscera,* and many other books and magazines. He's also the editor of the anthologies *Eros Ex Machina: Eroticizing the Mechanica, Midsummer Night's Dreams: One Story, Many Tales, Guilty Pleasures: True Tales of Erotic Indulgences, Rough Stuff: Tales of Gay Men, Sex and Power,* and *The Burning Pen: Sex Writers on Sex Writing.* His collection, *Dirty Words: A Collection of Provocative Erotica* is forthcoming from Alyson Books.

LEO CULLEN was born in Co Tipperary and now lives in Dublin. He has had short stories broadcast on BBC and Irish radio, and has been published in many magazines. He is the author of a book of fiction, *Clocking Ninety on the Road to Cloughjordan* (Blackstaff Press, 1994). In 1996 he was awarded a bursary by the Irish Arts Council, and is presently writing a novel.

MAYA DAVIS is the pseudonym for a writer living and working in Vancouver, B.C. She's a straightish girl who writes erotic stories as a release from more mundane business communications.

DEAN DURBER lives in Sydney, Australia, where he writes for a spectrum of publications. Children's stories. Gay erotica. Anarchistic commentary. Where does it all connect? Through his fiction, which is written primarily for his own sanity. And to speak of the misunderstood complexities of what lies beneath his rather attractive body.

ERIN GRAHAM is, among other things, a Vancouver writer, actor, and mental health worker. She used to compete in powerlifting competitions and still likes to heave around large amounts of black iron. She grew up in Alberta, but she seems to have a kind of Maritime accent, and what's up with that?

KRISTINE HAWES is currently one of the fiction editors for *Clean Sheets*, an online erotica webzine. She's published numerous poems in the U.S. and Canada, and her first book of poetry, *Cascades of Silence: The Café Leviticus Poems* (Alternate Way Press), was published in 1996. Her first erotic story, "Wanting You My Way," appeared in *Batteries Not Included* (Masquerade Press, 1999). She lives and works in San Jose, California.

JANICE J. HEISS lives in San Francisco. Her writing has appeared in various publications, including *The Ecstatic Moment: The Best of Libido, Frontiers, Women's Words, The Lullwater Review, Herotica 2,* and *First Person Sexual* (both under a pseudonym), and *Sex Spoken Here,* etc.

ROBERT LABELLE is a graduate of Concordia University's Masters program in creative writing. His work has been seen in the literary compilations, *Queer View Mirror* and *Quickies: Short Short Fiction on Gay Male Desire,* as well as Montreal's new writing magazines, *Fish Piss* and *Sugar Diet*.

ANDI MATHIS is the pseudonym of a white, working class, New York lesbian who loves learning, writing, *Xena,* and the poetry of Marilyn Hacker. Her work has appeared in numerous anthologies. She is currently working on a novel about Canada, geology, and starting over.

ROBIN METCALFE has been a sleeping-car porter, gay journalist and art critic. Published in seven countries and four languages, he has received two Canada Council "B" grants and is the author of *Studio Rally: Art and Craft of Nova Scotia*. He works as an independent curator in Halifax. "The Shirt" first appeared in *Mandate* magazine (August 1984) and was reprinted in *Flesh and the Word: An Anthology of Erotic Writing,* edited by John Preston (NAL Dutton/Penguin, 1992) and in *The Second Gates of Paradise: The Anthology of Erotic Short Fiction,* edited by Alberto Manguel (Macfarlane Walter & Ross, 1994). Reprinted with permission of the author.

STEVE NUGENT lives in Toronto. He has contributed to *fab* maga-
zine, the *Church-Wellesley Review, Eye Magazine, Lambda Book
Report, FAB National,* and *Quickies 2: Short Short Fiction on Gay Male
Desire.*

STAN PERSKY is the author of *Autobiography of a Tattoo, Buddy's,* and
Then We Take Berlin, and teaches philosophy and political studies at
Capilano College in North Vancouver, B.C. He also hosts the popular
Philosopher's Café discussion series, and writes the column
"Europa" for the *Vancouver Sun.* "Autobiography of a Tattoo (2: The
Barracks)" is reprinted with permission of New Star Books.

INA PROEBER chose writing as her vocation three years ago and discovered that fiction and creative non-fiction suited her most. She
likes to spin a tale and let the experiences of her years travelling
emerge in her short stories. Now having settled with husband and
dog, she is writing her memoirs.

THOMAS S. ROCHE is the editor of the *Noirotica* series of erotic
crime-noir-mystery anthologies. Some of his short stories are collected in *Dark Matter.* He publishes a newsletter, *Razorblade
Valentines,* about his work; to subscribe, email thomasroche-
announce-subscribe@onelist.com or visit www.thomasroche.com.

LAWRENCE SCHIMEL is twenty-eight years old and lives in Madrid,
where he's a full-time author and anthologist. A born New Yorker,
he's published over forty books, including *The Drag Queen of Elfland,
Switch Hitters: Lesbians Write Gay Male Erotica and Gay Men Write
Lesbian Erotica* (with Carol Queen), *Boy Meets Boy, The Mammoth
Book of Gay Erotica,* and *PoMoSexuals: Challenging Assumptions About
Gender and Sexuality* (with Carol Queen), among others. His work
has been translated into sixteen other languages. His web page is
www.circlet.com/schimel.html.

MARCY SHEINER is editor of the *Herotica* series, *The Oy of Sex: Jewish Women Write Erotica*, and *Best Women's Erotica 2000*, due out in March 2000. She is also Erotica Editor for *The Position.com*, the site for the Museum of Sex. Her essays, reviews and stories have appeared in numerous magazines and anthologies. She is currently working on a novel and a collection of essays about motherhood.

SIMON SHEPPARD is the co-editor, with M. Christian, of *Rough Stuff: Tales of Gay Men, Sex and Power*, and the author of the forthcoming *Hotter Than Hell and Other Stories*, both from Alyson Books. His work has appeared in numerous anthologies, including *The Best American Erotica 2000* and *1997*, and four editions of *Best Gay Erotica*. He lives in San Francisco, and hasn't been to Rome in a while.

JEAN SMITH is the author of two novels, *I Can Hear Me Fine* (Get To The Point Publishing) and *The Ghost Of Understanding* (Arsenal Pulp Press), but is probably better known as the singer in the duo Mecca Normal. She is currently at work on a solo album. Jean lives with herself in Vancouver, without houseplants or pets. "What about that aloe plant?" "Shut up."

RON SMITH was born and raised in Vancouver and now lives in Lantzville on Vancouver Island. His writing has appeared in magazines in Australia, Canada, England, Italy, Jugoslavia, and the United States. He is the author of three books of poetry. "Desire" is from his collection of stories, *What Men Know About Women* (Oolichan, 1999), reprinted with permission of the author.

KAREN X. TULCHINSKY is the award-winning author of *Love Ruins Everything* and *In Her Nature*. She is the editor of eight anthologies, including the best-selling *Hot & Bothered: Short Short Fiction on Lesbian Desire (1* and *2)*, and *Friday the Rabbi Wore Lace: Jewish Lesbian Erotica*. She teaches creative writing and writes for numerous magazines. She lives in Vancouver, B.C.

MICHELE DAVIDSON lives in Vancouver. She writes erotica under a pseudonym. *Exhibitions* is her first anthology. She considers sex to be one of life's grand adventures, and believes erotica should be compulsory bedtime reading for adults. Although Michele loves her work as a fundraising and communications consultant for environmental organizations, her dream is one day to do this part time and write and travel the rest. An avid outdoorswoman, Michele's next project is a collection of mountaineering stories.

DEBBIE STOLLER is the co-founder, co-publisher, and Editorial Director of *BUST* magazine. She recently co-edited *The BUST Guide to the New Girl Order* (Viking Penguin). Debbie has written about women and pop culture for a variety of publications, including *George*, *Ms.*, *The Village Voice*, and *New York Newsday*, among others, and also pens a column about women and pop culture, "The XX Files," for *Shift Online* (www.shift.com) She holds a Ph.D. in the Psychology of Women from Yale University.

Sex and Erotica Books
from Arsenal Pulp Press

These books and others published by Arsenal Pulp Press are available at better bookstores, or directly from the press prepaid (please add shipping charges of $3.00 for the first book, and $1.50 per book thereafter, plus 7% GST in Canada).

ARSENAL PULP PRESS
103, 1014 Homer Street
Vancouver, BC
Canada V6B 2W9

Books can also be ordered by calling, toll-free, 1-888-600-PULP, or visit our website, **www.arsenalpulp.com**.

THE BALD-HEADED HERMIT
& THE ARTICHOKE
AN EROTIC THESAURUS
compiled by A.D. Peterkin

A unique guide to the lingo of sex, compiling over 15,000 terms relating to all aspects of human sexuality, from breasts and penises, to fetishes, paraphernalia, and specific erotic practices.

"Excellent. . . . In a word, The Bald-Headed Hermit *& the Artichoke is a hoot."* – Libido

$13.95 US / $16.95 Canada

COMING IN SEPTEMBER 2000
CARNAL NATION
NEW SEX FICTIONS
edited by Carellin Brooks & Brett Josef Grubisic

An intoxicating anthology of writing about sex by an exciting new generation of writers, *CARNAL NATION* collects stories about sex by writers who boldly push the narrative envelope. These are not your typical bump-and-grind tales, but stories written in a startling new language.

$16.95 US / $19.95 Canada

HOT & BOTHERED
SHORT SHORT FICTION ON LESBIAN DESIRE
edited by Karen X. Tulchinsky

Sensuous tales of seduction, wistful fantasies about co-workers, hot encounters between strangers: storeis written to get you *hot & bothered*. Sixty-nine writers from eight different countries contribute to *HOT & BOTHERED*, a collection of "short short fiction" that explores the infinite possibilities of sexual desire between women. From public piercings, to lesbian vampires, to hot sex between long-term lovers, these imaginative, uninhibited stories will delight, arouse, and inspire you in 1,000 words or less.

"Hot, sexy, and intelligent." – Diva

$14.95 US / $16.95 Canada

QUICKIES
SHORT SHORT FICTION ON GAY MALE DESIRE
edited by James C. Johnstone

They can be anything, and happen anywhere: shy glances across crowded rooms; unspoken encounters in dark corners. In the sauna, under the bridge, down in the stripping room: quickies. In these hot, uninhibited examples of "short short fiction," sixty-nine writers from seven different countries depict, in 1,000 words or less, the geography of gay male desire, from first kiss to last calls; there are cigar angels, true cowboys, and the kind of raw mansex that will challenge and inspire you.

"Quickies may be a fast read; however, the stories collected will stay on your mind for a long time to come." – Lambda Book Report

$14.95 US / $16.95 Canada

HOT & BOTHERED 2
SHORT SHORT FICTION ON LESBIAN DESIRE
edited by Karen X. Tulchinsky

Interested in getting even more hot and bothered? This second volume continues where the first left off: sensual tales of lesbian desire, seduction, and fantasy. Included are stories by sixty-nine-plus writers from numerous countries whose beguiling stories will arouse and inspire you.

> *"This volume of* Hot & Bothered *is sure to be as popular as the last."* – Lambda Book Report

> *$14.95 US / $17.95 Canada*

QUICKIES 2
SHORT SHORT FICTION ON GAY MALE DESIRE
edited by James C. Johnstone

Just what the doctor ordered: another dose of quickies. This second volume, which includes sixty-nine-lus writers from numerous countries, delivers some of the hottest tales yet, from furtive glances to anonymous encounters. These new *Quickies* will take you on a wild ride.

> *"Bound to become a must-have for any home library."* – Outlooks

> *$14.95 US / $17.95 Canada*